# Krampus Comes to Town

Jeff Chapman

Krampus Comes to Town
Jeff Chapman

Cover image by Nicky from Pixabay.

# Chapter One
# Four Days to Christmas

Hans leaned into the rope looped round his waist. The cord slipped above his hips to dig through his winter coat and woolen sweater into the softer flesh around his stomach, like a tourniquet twisting to cut him in two. Ice cracked and snapped behind him, with great reluctance giving up its hold on the wooden sled's runners. Bags of flour, sugar, and oatmeal and two bundles his parents didn't know about were strapped to the sled. He imagined lines of stress spreading through the weakening ice like spindly fingers squeezing to crush it.

"Push, Helga. Push."

"I'm. Trying." His sister's voice stretched thin with strain. Her boots sank in the snow and the hem of her woolen dress dragged across the crystalline powder.

Hans stopped pulling and panted open-mouthed with his tongue lolling out over his teeth. Ahead, fifty yards up the snow-doused slope, the crest of the ridge beckoned. Fifty more yards of pulling to an easy ride down the other side.

The path ahead cut between stands of larch and spruce. Sharp edges were soft curves under snow, just as water curves over sharp rocks in a fast stream. Cracking his head on one of those rocks would split his skull. Must be careful not to slip, he thought. Blood dyed snow a very dark red.

Above, the bare branches of the larches topped with snow recalled sweet, chewy twists of cinnamon bread dusted with powdered sugar. Snow muffled boulders appeared no more formidable than mounds of straw, easy work for a pitchfork.

Snow weighed on the spruce branches, tightening their conical forms, reminding him of the arrow tips he used for archery. His spirits swelled at the thought of the new bow he hoped to find under the tree.

A snowflake struck his tongue. It was wet and tasteless. Another glided along his nose, and a third crashed into his left eyelashes. He blinked and brushed his mitten across his eye. The flakes came out of nowhere, invisible against the gray sky.

On either side of the pass, the snow clouds smothered the peaks of the Three Sisters, the three-headed mountain that guarded the valley. Masses of dark gray rock, riven with fissures, disappeared into the mist. How a vapor could blot out the mighty rocks of the earth seemed wrong to Hans. A single drop of water tickled the end of his nose. He swiped at it. His breath turned to frost like steam from a little train huffing and puffing.

Hans put one foot forward, compressing a soft layer of fresh powder before crunching through an older, frozen layer, searching for leverage.

"We should have gone through the village," said Helga.

"Father would have seen us. They must be surprises."

"Not if we're buried and freeze to death."

Hans ignored her. The surprise didn't matter so much, but he had set out on this course and he intended to finish it. The men of his family were stiff and stubborn, his mother oft repeated. He was determined to follow the path he had begun to the end.

It had been Helga's idea to stop and rest. Girls were like that. And now they were frozen stuck and working against a snowstorm. A sudden gust roared down the slope and peppered Hans's face with pellets of frozen snow. The end of his scarf flapped behind him and a sliver of wind found an ample chink below his stocking cap to whistle in his ear.

Hans felt something solid beneath his boot. Maybe a rock. He leaned against the rope. The sled broke free with a cracking lurch. Hans sprang forward and fell face-first into a snow drift.

"We did it. We did it." Helga was laughing, jumping. The pair of braids peeking out beneath her stocking cap bounced.

Hans took a breath and filled his mouth with ice crystals. He wheezed as his throat constricted, his lungs failing to draw air. He raised his head only to suck in more melting snow and fill his mouth and nose with ice water.

The sled didn't matter. His sister didn't matter. Nothing but air mattered. He was drowning on the side of a mountain.

He flailed his arms, jabbing at the snow for leverage, but all he found was soft powder. His heart pounded in his head. With a furious kick, his left foot found purchase. He twisted over onto his back.

He lay still and gasped until he'd filled his lungs with cold air. Ice crystals stuck to his eyebrows. His skin felt scraped and wet where a thin layer of the snow had melted on contact. He dried his face on his coat sleeve. Cold, wet skin frozen in the wind was dangerous.

"Hans, are you hurt?"

He sat up, coughed, and sneezed. "I'm fine. Why didn't you pull me out?" He brushed snow from his stocking cap. "You could have grabbed my coat."

"I didn't know you were stuck. You fell down and then you rolled over."

He realized what seemed several minutes to him might have lasted only a few seconds.

A clucking sound drew his attention to the trees farther up the slope.

"Quiet." Hans listened, all his senses focused on the stand of spruce and larches.

"What is it?" whispered Helga.

"I don't know. Sounded like—" It couldn't be. "Like laughter."

"Echoes from a branch snapping?"

"Maybe."

"A mouse could roar like a lion up here. All the echoes."

Hans studied the spruce and larches. His nerves stood on edge. Shadows crowded among the trees at ground level. Anyone or anything could hide there and watch them. Another gust of wind swirled snow over the crest of the ridge and whistled through the trees, animating the shadows.

*When you're in the mountains, ignoring your instincts will bring you peril.* His father's oft-repeated words echoed in his head.

Hans grinned. "Could be Old Krampus gathering firewood for his next feast."

"Let's go back, Hans. You're scaring me."

"We've gone too far. Krampus isn't after good children." Hans struggled to his feet in the snow, sinking to his knees in the drift. For a moment the trees and mountain wavered, refusing to hold still. Hans's head spun. He tilted to-and-fro. The snow gripping his calves held him upright until the dizziness passed.

"Hans, are you sick?"

"I'm fine. I'm fine. We're going to freeze down again." Hans leaned into the rope. The cord tightened. The runners hissed, sliding over snow. One long burst and they would be at the top. "Push."

"Umph," cried his sister.

The rope slackened for an instant around his hips as he kicked through the drift, raising a powdery cloud to join the snowflakes falling from the sky. He charged forward, stepping through the snow which now came only to the top of his boots. Momentum favored him.

With single-minded determination, Hans eyed the top of the ridge. It stretched from the base of one peak to another, like a rope stretched between two trees. The snow curved gently over the crest of the ridge, rising up one slope of the mountain and falling down the other. Each step brought him closer. Each breath gave him a surge of energy. He kicked through another drift without a glance at the shadowy trees.

His sister cried out but he ignored her. He'd deal with her problem later. Her girlish shrieks had no bearing on the last few yards to the top. A few more yards and they would scream with elation at the thrill of hissing down the slope toward home.

A shadow moved on his left, coming out of the trees. Its arm swung toward him. He debated running ahead and paying the shadow no heed. He was so close. Shadows were of no consequence, tricks of the light at best. If the shape was a branch that had fallen, he should run faster, climb higher, but Helga was behind him, below the fallen branch. Hans looked to his left without pausing his headlong charge.

Johan stood in the snow in front of the trees.

Where had Johan come from? The boy was a half-foot taller than Hans and one-and-a-half again as wide. Equal parts glee and derision animated his ugly grin. Johan the Terrible they called him, the terror of the schoolyard.

Johan wore his red plaid hat lined with sheepskin, the sewn-in ear muffs turned down. The hat had been the previous year's Christmas present and, if rumor held any truth, Johan's only present for some years. The boy's father drank to forget his lost wife. Johan's clothes carried the reek of schnapps. A constant reminder. Johan gripped a branch the thickness of a man's leg in both hands. His elbows locked as he swept the limb toward Hans.

The branch caught Hans across his gut. It cracked like a clap of jagged thunder when it snapped. Bits of black, rotting bark littered the snow.

Hans doubled over, all his wind forced out like someone stomping on a bellows. The broken branch tangled with his ankles, sending him skidding into the snow toward the trees. His skid stopped when his head thumped a snow-covered rock the size of a suckling pig.

The hollow clop of his skull contacting the rock made him feel sick. He wheezed. He groaned. A sharp pain creased his abdomen.

His sister was shouting. Snow crunched under her rapid footfalls.

"Hans? Hans? You hurt him. You brute."

"Shut up." Johan's voice had already broken and deepened. He sounded like a man. His words carried the extra weight of a blacksmith's hammer.

Hans probed the top of his head through his stocking cap. A painful knot had risen. It was hard, the shape and size of an acorn, as if someone had planted one under his skin. What a strange notion, he thought. He was curled tight, testing the edges of the knot, when a boot caught his upper arm and rolled him onto his back.

Through a haze of snowflakes, Johan grinned down on him. The boy's blue eyes gleamed with the brightness of a summer sky. He took pleasure in other's pain. Johan raised his boot. Scuffs scarred the sole. Wet nail heads rimmed the edge. Hans watched the boot grow as Johan brought it down on his breast bone.

Hans found his chest would not expand as Johan compressed his ribs. Hans grabbed Johan's ankle in both hands. He struggled to lift it but the angles were all wrong and his leverage weak.

Johan held the advantage in weight and strength. Hans's heart raced. Johan was mean but the brute wouldn't kill him, would he?

"Stop it." With her arms raised over her head, Helga beat on Johan's shoulder. A short girl, her head reached no higher than Johan's ribs. "Stop it. You're hurting him."

Johan swung his arm, catching the girl in her armpit and flinging her toward the sled. "Get off me, you stupid girl."

Helga flew backward. Her wide eyes attesting to her surprise at being air born. She landed with a grunt behind the sled.

Hans wanted nothing more than to land one solid blow on Johan's mouth and knock out a tooth for Helga. He may have despised his little sister at times, but no one insulted his family. Fury tapped his last well of strength. He dug his thumbs under the toe and heel of Johan's boot, searching for better leverage. His gloved thumbs slipped on the cold, wet surface. If he could wedge his palms under the boot and twist, he might shift it off his chest.

The pressure on his chest eased enough to allow a wheezing breath. His starved lungs ached from the sudden influx of cold air. The scent of wet leather and rotting larch needles filled Hans's nose. His gaze met Johan's. A cold, wicked joy burned bright in his tormentor's eyes, like the blue in the ice of a glacier.

Johan pressed down again. Hans struggled against the boot. Helga sobbed and sat up in the snow.

"I want a favor from you," said Johan.

What? Hans doubted his hearing. He managed to hiss one word with his remaining breath. "Favor?"

Johan moved his foot to the ground and crunched snow beneath it.

"That's what I said. You got snow in your ears? I'll want your help soon and I want to know I'll get it."

Hans sat up, taking in all the cold mountain air he could inhale. He still wanted to fight, but he had to breathe first.

Helga crawled to her feet. Hans followed her gaze to the length of branch which had broken across Hans. It was the perfect length for a club and lay between them and the sled. He liked his sister's thinking.

"Sit down, girl." Johan's voice boomed with the commanding authority of their father's.

Helga plopped back into the snow as if Johan had struck her down.

"Do what?" said Hans. "Why would we do anything for you?"

Johan loomed over him like a black storm cloud coming down the mountains. He grasped the loose folds of Hans's coat covering his shoulder. Johan's breath smelled of sausage and onions, but the reek of stale schnapps came at him like the leading edge of an avalanche and buried him in its scent. It was a warm smell but without comfort. More than once, he'd seen Johan's father stumbling through the village, bleary-eyed and flushed, the gendarme gripping his arm.

Johan lifted Hans by his coat. A seam bit into his underarm. All thoughts of fighting left him. Johan's strength frightened him. Hans had never been in a fight before, not like this, not with real physical injury a certainty. The gendarme manhandled Johan's drunken father and now Johan was manhandling him.

Johan's eyes narrowed, his lips curled back from yellow teeth. Meanness wafted from him like smoke from a smoldering fire. A snowflake rested on the brim of Johan's hat, symmetrical and delicate with precise angles like the ones Hans created at school with folded paper and scissors. How could beauty abide someone so ugly?

Johan gave Hans a vicious jerk, snapping his head against his shoulder. "I'll tell you when you need to know. You understand?"

Hans nodded.

"Good." Johan dropped him to the ground. He grabbed the front of Hans's stocking cap and yanked it down past his chin.

Hans struggled to pull his cap off. The yarn stretched tight, catching on his chin and nose. Snow crunched under Johan's steps.

"Leave those alone," said his sister.

Hans yanked his cap off. The cold bit his sweaty hair. Johan was bent over their sled, tugging on something. Paper ripped.

Johan turned to Hans. He held the two small bundles which had been tied on top of the flour and sugar.

"I'll keep these for now."

"Those are for Christmas," said Hans.

"You'll get 'em back in time," said Johan. "If you do what I say."

Hans eyed the broken branch beside the sled. The humiliation of the cap and now the theft of the gifts had fired his anger. He and Helga had no more money for gifts. They had spent it all. Maybe he could snatch up the branch when Johan turned his back. He imagined whacking Johan over the head. The image felt good, like redemption, like revenge.

Johan looked at the branch as if he'd heard Hans's thoughts.

"You runt bastard." Johan kicked the branch, sending it flying end over end, trailing bits of bark, toward the larches, where it disappeared in a snow drift. "You cross me and I'll bust your nose and send your teeth home with you in your pocket." Vapor and spittle puffed from his mouth like an over-heating kettle.

Hans nodded. The last of the fight left him. Snowflakes landed on his short-cropped hair. They melted. The water trickled down his forehead. Today was not the day to win this war. Helga whimpered. Hans sniffed, fighting to hold back his own emotions.

Johan crunched through the snow, making for the larches. He followed us from the village, thought Hans, and caught up with us when Helga insisted we rest.

"Go ahead and cry," said Johan. "Run home to your mama. But if you tell her about me, you'll never see these." He shook the packages. "I'll burn them."

Hans watched Johan's shadow disappear among the shadows of the trees. Helga was wailing. Impotent hatred burned in his chest.

JOHAN FOUND HIS FATHER Karl slumped over a wooden plate at the table where they ate their meals, or would have, if they had eaten regular meals. Father and son ate when they were hungry with no regard for the other. A knife with a handle made from deer antler protruded from a quarter wedge of cheese on a cutting board. Beside the cheese was a quarter loaf of black bread.

Neither father nor son cooked. They survived on cheese, bread, and sausage supplemented with radishes and onions. Customers sometimes paid in kind with a pot of stew. Johan washed the clay and wooden dishes when there were no clean ones left in the cupboard. Karl threw dishes when he was angry.

Their shattered remains littered the floor near the walls. Johan found himself washing dishes more often.

When Johan's father was sober or only a little drunk, he cut and dressed stone, the only stonemason for several leagues. Everyone knew to see him in the morning. By late afternoon, he was of no use.

Karl's broad shoulders capped a heavily muscled chest. His head rested across the plate as if he were being served as the meal, his mouth agape. The only piece missing was an apple in his mouth. Deep snores escaped between his yellow teeth. His hands were thick and calloused. His right arm lay bent across the table and in the long-necked shadow of a bottle of schnapps. His fingers curled round a wooden cup.

The fire had dwindled. In the flickering orange glow, Johan could not discern if any drink remained in the bottle. He didn't dare sip from it. His father was prone to waking without warning. Foul moods followed. The burly man had caught Johan with a bottle once and beat him to within an inch of his life with a broken broom handle. Karl had called Johan a thief and chased the boy around the cottage until his rage was spent and they had both collapsed, Johan with painful welts across his back and arms, his father in drunken exhaustion. Karl jealously guarded his precious drink. He did not share.

If Johan was lucky, his father would sleep like this for hours, wake long enough to finish the bottle, and then stumble to his bed in the back room where he would likely piss himself. Johan slept in a loft. He always pulled up the ladder.

Johan no longer smelled the schnapps. The scent had permeated every bit of wood and cloth in the two-room cottage. He reached for the knife and cut a slice of cheese.

He stood beside the table while he chewed it and watched the dying fire. He felt confident Hans would obey him and the sister would follow along, whimpering. Survival was all that mattered, and he would pay whatever cost it required.

Johan's father grunted. Johan snatched the bread, hiding it behind his back. He stepped away from the table, well out of reach. Karl sat upright, panting as if he'd run a race. Johan eyed the white handled knife resting atop the yellow cheese. He should have taken the knife, not the bread. He calculated the risks of grabbing the blade and exposing his presence or waiting for the alcohol to pull his father back to sleep. Johan stood still as a stone. The coarse bread compressed and crumbled in his tightening grasp.

Karl blinked and shook his head like a wet dog. He rubbed his face with his left hand and ran his fingers through his greasy, unkempt hair. He looked at his right hand. His eyebrows arched. He seemed surprised to find a cup in his hand. He found the bottle and poured. Nothing came out.

"Damn."

Johan inched farther from the table and the fire, moving into the shadows. His boots scraped across the gritty floorboards which had long forgotten the caress of a broom.

His father turned on him. "You! Don't you address your father, boy?"

"Evening, father."

"Better." He belched. "Now fetch me another bottle. And make your legs quick about it. Your father shouldn't—" Another belch. "Shouldn't have to wait."

Johan opened the cupboard where the schnapps lived. A full bottle. Please, a full bottle, he said to himself. A full bottle would make his father happy and he would drink until he slept. Johan found four bottles laying on their sides, not a cork among them. He felt around the back and corners where he couldn't see. His fingers scraped rough wood and tangled in cobwebs. The empty bottles rolled at the least touch and clinked together, laughing at him.

"Where's my schnapps? And put some wood on the fire. You useless piece of crap. I'm freezing."

With his back to his father, Johan stretched his mouth around the bread and bit. He chewed while he searched the neighboring cupboards.

His father banged his cup on the table. "Too slow. You're too slow."

"All the bottles are empty."

"What? Someone steals from me. A thief stalks this village. Do I know who it is?"

Johan pressed his back to the cupboards. As far from the table as possible. The knife remained in the cheese.

Karl pointed a finger at Johan. Sweat caught in his beard glistened in the firelight. His other fingers and thumb gripped the cup. "You drank it. Didn't you, boy? Don't lie to your father."

Johan recognized the crazy look in his father's eyes. He stepped sideways, sliding along the cupboards. He shook his head. "No. I didn't. I swear."

Karl rose from his chair. Johan was big for his age but his father was large for any age, a foot taller than most men in the village. Before he straightened his knees he lost his balance and collapsed backward. The chair tipped, on the verge of keeling over, but Karl lunged for the table and the chair followed.

He groaned, kneading his forehead with his empty hand. The joints in the chair creaked.

Karl shook his head. Johan stilled, likening his father to stags he had seen in the woods, rallying their strength to charge another stag. Karl cocked his arm and threw the cup into the hearth. The wooden vessel cracked against the stones at the back of the fireplace. Splintered pieces of cup soaked in years of alcohol showered the fire. Flames leapt to eat the new fuel.

Father and son stared at one another, each taking the measure of the other. The fire crackled with consuming the cup.

He's going to kill me someday, thought Johan. Someday he'll forget who I am and crush my neck. Johan couldn't bring himself to hate his father, not enough to kill him first. Blood was a thick and forgiving binder, resistant to breaking. Johan found it far easier to hate Hans and Helga and all the other children in the village.

Karl fiddled with the top button on his trousers. He pulled out a soft leather pouch. The purse was lashed to his belt, but he kept it tucked inside his pants, fearful someone would steal from him during a drunken slumber. Johan doubted any disturbance would wake his father when he was fully drunk. Karl's precautions with the coin purse bothered Johan the most about his father's drinking. Even in fits of sobriety, his father planned for his drunken eventuality.

Karl loosened the cord that cinched the purse. Coins clinked as his fingers rooted through them. He moved his lower jaw from side to side. His grizzled beard twitched with the movement.

"Cut me some cheese, boy."

Johan thrust the bread into the outer pocket of his coat as he approached the table. He didn't relish the proximity to his father but at least he would be holding the knife. His father was most apt to anger when he was somewhere in between sober and dead-to-the-world drunk. Johan grasped the handle. His hand conformed to the smooth bone and its ridges as if it were made for him. His father did not appear to fear him, never worried Johan might harm him. Johan felt weak in his father's presence. He removed the knife and cut a thick slice.

"Ah." His father retrieved a thick silver piece and held it out to Johan. "Go to the tavern. Tell Heinrich I want two bottles. Talk only to Heinrich. Hear me?"

Johan nodded, shoving the coin into his pocket with the bread. This instruction about Heinrich was new. Why? He hesitated to ask. And what if he could not find Heinrich? Coming home without the schnapps was akin to begging for a beating. He dropped the knife at the far end of the table, out of his father's reach.

"You be careful now. Don't tarry in the dark patches. I saw him in the moonlight two nights ago and I've heard him snuffling around the door."

"Who?"

"Krampus. He's overdue for a visit. Decades hence. And wouldn't he like to sink his claws into a nasty boy like you?"

Johan's eyes widened. He figured his father would turn him over to the monster in the blink of an eye if it profited him a drink.

Karl grinned and then laughed. "Don't piss yourself with fear. Off with you!" He snatched up the empty bottle by its neck and brandished it like a cudgel.

Johan scurried toward the door, scattering a pile of broken crockery in his haste.

HANS WATCHED HIS FATHER'S black king jump the last three red pieces on the board. Click. Click. Clunk. The king kissed the black squares and then stopped his murdering rampage.

Hans's father tilted his chair on its back legs and drummed his fingers on his abdomen. Creases stretched from the corners of his mouth, enlarging his smile. He cocked his head and raised his eyebrows.

"Three games in a row and I'm not even trying."

Hans shrugged. For years the checkerboard had been their battleground, the place where the son proved himself. No quarter was given. He couldn't tell his father why his heart wasn't in the game.

From the moment Johan had left them, Hans had been focused on where to find those presents. He didn't figure Johan would take them home, so they must be hidden in a cache in one of the Three Sisters' peaks. Find the presents and Johan would have no hold over Hans and his sister.

"Getting that goose egg must have rattled something loose in your head. What say you, Greta?"

His mother and sister rocked in a pair of chairs as they knitted. The creaking of the chairs joined with the clacking of their needles to rival the snapping of the fire in the hearth. His mother was knitting a sweater, his sister at work on mittens. The creaking of one of the chairs ceased.

Greta lay her knitting atop her yarn basket, her steps in her soft-soled slippers a mere whisper. Their cat Snowball stretched on his side with his back to the hearth stone, soaking up the heat, storing warmth for a night of mousing. His green eyes followed Hans's mother.

Hans winced when his mother touched the knot rising like an incipient goat horn from the crest of his head. He scrunched his neck to escape her touch as her fingers probed the lump's edges.

"I daresay it's not grown any worse. Does it still pain you?"

"A little," Hans lied. Truth was, his head throbbed with dull pain, and his worrying over the fate of the presents did nothing to ease it. There were caves in the mountain and countless fissures in the rock face. There wasn't time to search every one of them.

"I think your mind was already addled." The front legs of his father's chair thumped against the floor. His arms landed on the table and sent a stack of red checkers falling across the board like a gout of spilled blood. "What demon possessed you to haul a fully loaded sled up the mountain to slide down. Would have been a miracle if you hadn't fallen off and knocked your head."

"Franz, don't. He's already suffered."

"It was my idea," Helga mumbled.

"What?" said Franz. "You?"

Helga's attention never left her knitting and the needles clacked faster. To match the building rhythm of her heart, Hans speculated.

"I— I—" Helga stuttered.

"Don't hide your face," said Franz.

Helga raised her head. "I thought we would go faster. All the supplies."

Hans appreciated his sister's well-meant intervention, but in his father's eyes, the only crime worse than doing something stupid was doing something stupid at the urging of someone else.

"Is that true, Hans? I'd expect you to exercise more good sense."

"Franz. Stop scolding the children. They know they made a mistake and they won't do it again. Will you?"

"No," the children answered in unison.

"We should be thanking sweet mother Mary they were not seriously hurt. Or the flour and meal spilled."

Hans hugged his mother and pressed his head into the wool of her dress, convinced that the only barrier to a trip to the woodshed was his mother's skirts.

With one eye he peeked from behind the folds of material at his sister. Helga pleaded with her eyes for him to tell the truth. Hans shook his head.

He had insisted Helga promise on her rosary not to tell about Johan. It had not occurred to Hans or Helga that swearing on a rosary to lie to their parents might be a conflict. Hans was ashamed the bully had beaten him. He feared his father in a fit of anger would assault the stonemason or call in the gendarme. It was best to leave adults out of these battles.

His mother brushed the back of his head with her strong fingers. His father sighed in the face of religion and thankfulness for blessings. The threat of further punishment had passed. Only his head would pain Hans this night.

A rap at the door startled all four of them. Snowball was on his paws with his ears pointed at the door before its rattling reverberations ceased.

Hans's mother asked the obvious question. The feet of Franz's chair scraped across the floor as he pushed it back from the table. The legs scraped with resistance and reluctance, thought Hans, like an old ewe digging in her hooves before the butcher's blade.

Franz didn't answer his wife's question, at least not with words. He stalked through the main room—which served for cooking, dining, and family bonding—and then through the parlor. The door rattled under a second assault.

"Who calls?"

Nighttime visitors rarely troubled their threshold and their news was seldom cheery unless someone had given birth. Hans knew of no neighbors with child. The gravelly voice of Klaus Reich, the owner of the neighboring farm, raked the peace of their evening.

Klaus did not accept the offer to enter. The yellow light of a lantern curled round the door's edge. Franz stepped outside, closing the door behind.

"What does Herr Reich want?" said Helga.

"I don't know," said Greta. "Perchance one of his cows is sick."

Franz was highly regarded for his healing skills with animals.

Greta crossed to a window and pulled aside the heavy gray curtain. Hans followed. A lantern bobbed in the farmyard, disappeared inside the barn, and then emerged to circle behind the building.

"They're checking the stock," said Hans.

"Appears so," said his mother.

"Wolves," said Hans. "A pack has come out of the forest." He spoke with excited relish, forgetting the threat of Johan for the moment. Hans welcomed anything to upset the boring rhythm of their lives. "Or a bear."

"We will pray not," said Greta.

"Are the animals safe?" said Helga.

"Your father built a sturdy barn," said Greta.

"There will be a hunt," said Hans.

"On which you will not go," said Greta. "Far too dangerous."

Hans expected his father would have a different opinion. Franz would want him to begin taking his place among the men. He hoped. He considered what extra chores he could do to raise his father's good opinion.

"They're coming back," said Greta.

The lantern bobbed across the yard toward the house. Klaus held the lantern loosely and his arm was slack, so the lantern swung freely with his stride and only illuminated the men's legs.

Greta let the curtain fall. She and Hans waited before the table, watching the door and listening. Voices murmured outside in low, hushed tones, the words indistinct. To approach the door and press an ear to the crack between the door and frame would stretch beyond the pale of family trust.

His mother bit her lip and squeezed Hans's shoulder. Helga resumed her chair and clacked away with her needles, striving to knit normality back into their lives. Hans squeezed the edge of the table. Such a hunt, an opportunity to prove himself, might not come again for years. The elusive mantle of manhood dangled out of arm's reach if only he could step past his mother's skirts.

A frown turned down the corners of Franz's mouth when he entered the cottage. He secured the door and rattled it to test the strength of the stout wooden bar.

"What is it, Franz?" said Greta.

Franz strode past them to his chair at the table. He met Greta's gaze and then Hans's but said nothing as he chewed on his thoughts. Helga's needles clacked with more urgency as if each of her father's footfalls rent the tear in the fabric of their lives a little wider. Franz's chair creaked under his weight.

"Something has been killing livestock. The Hauptmanns lost three hens. The Hoenigs lost their Christmas pig. The Reichs lost two hens and a duck."

"You say—something," said Greta. "Were there no tracks?"

"None that make sense. And the sheds were ripped apart. Fetch my pipe, Hans."

Hans settled his sights on a bear. What else could rip a hole in a wall, tear planks from a frame with its bare paws? He brought the pipe and tobacco pouch to his father. Franz puffed when he wanted to think.

Greta took up her knitting in the rocking chair beside Helga and added her own measured rhythm to Helga's needle clacking. Hans picked up Snowball who protested with a meow before settling on Hans's lap as the boy stroked the cat's head and back. Franz tamped tobacco into the bowl of his pipe. He lit it from the taper burning on the table. Thick clouds of white smoke escaped his mouth, hiding his face until a warm draft whisked them to the ceiling.

"We found no damage to our coop or barn. Whatever it is hasn't visited us. We should replace Growler."

"A new puppy?" said Helga. Growler had been Helga's favorite and she had taken his death harder than anyone.

Franz guffawed, shooting a ball of smoke across the table. "We'll need more than a puppy. Herr Richter has a couple young mastiffs. He might sell me one if I make a good offer."

"What of the Reich's dog?" said Greta.

"Brained. With a board from the coop."

Helga gasped. Hans had never heard of a bear wielding a club. Were they hunting a man?

"A very good offer indeed. And quick. I'll see him in the morning."

"What good will the dog do against cunning?" said Greta.

"Sound the alarm if nothing more."

"Seems a great deal to spend for so little."

"In every war there's a sacrifice. It's an investment in the farm."

Hans's gaze shifted to his sister. Her needles were silent. Her gaze downcast. She's already grieving the dog, he thought.

"So it is a man who has done this?" said Greta.

"The tracks were hooves. Klaus said there's talk of Krampus."

Greta's gaze shifted between Hans and Helga. "No more forays up the Three Sisters for either of you until after Christmas. Do you hear?"

"Yes, mother." They answered in unison, their woeful chorus starkly out of place amid the festive spruce branches and red ribbon hung above the door and windows.

"You listen to your mother. If you don't, you'll wish Krampus had whipped you with his birch rods when I finish with you."

"Yes, father." Another mournful chorus, this time laced with fear.

Hans scratched Snowball's neck, searching for the edge of the cat's jaw, the sweet spot in the long fur. The cat raised his head, thrumming his appreciation.

If he didn't search the mountain for the presents, Hans reasoned, he was beholden to Johan and surely that was wrong. Krampus wouldn't hunt the children, and the bad ones at that, until Christmas eve. Pride held back admission of the fight. They had already lied. In Hans's mind, the bully was an indefatigable pillar of evil, something to carefully work around, like a crevice in a glacier. There's a middle course through this blizzard. Somewhere. He couldn't see it yet.

JOHAN PRESSED HIS BACK to the door of his cottage. The snow squall from earlier in the day had passed leaving a clear sky awash with stars. The lane was empty of travelers. Across it, candles lit the windows above the cabinet-maker's shop. Laughter permeated the glass, the tones of a happy family.

If he reached deep into his memory, he recalled a few happy times around their table when his mother was alive. Johan clenched his fists. Damn his little brother. Born dead and his mother bled to death, a sea of blood on the white sheets. His father had burned the bed, blankets and all.

The fresh snow glowed white and innocent in the gray light of a rising moon. Wind sweeping down the valley picked up snow crystals and flung them against clapboard. The tiny bits of snow were hard as sand.

Johan closed his eyes. His mother's face was visible on the cloudy fringes of his mind's eye. He saw her smiling, her soft blue eyes intent on him, and her blonde hair pulled back tight.

A heavy object shattered against the other side of the door. Johan leapt into the ruts of frozen slush between the shops and houses. Broken glass showered the floor behind the door, a sound he knew very well. Johan stared at the cottage. Did his father know he was there?

Johan trudged down the lane toward the tavern. The frozen slush crackled and crunched beneath his steps. He had much to consider. He passed the bakery, which always smelled of bread and strudel no matter the time of day. The yeasty aroma reminded him of the bread in his pocket. He chewed the crumbling handful of rye as he passed the butcher and the chandler across the lane.

There were dark and narrow alleyways between the buildings, perfect for concealing someone waiting in ambush. Johan stared down the dark passage between the butcher and the land surveyor's office. Would Krampus hide in the darkness here to snatch a child? No, Krampus wanted particular children, the very bad ones, like him. With the horns of a ram, the teeth of a wolf, and the tongue of a snake, Krampus would give anyone nightmares.

Johan wondered why his father had warned him. The old bastard would think it funny if Johan was too frightened to sleep.

A hiss and a growl filled the passage. Johan stood on his toes to snap an icicle off the butcher's roof. He sent it flying end-over-end into the darkness. There was a yowl as the ice cracked against something hollow and metal. A garbage bin for the offal, he figured.

Fearful the butcher would appear with club and cleaver to investigate, Johan hurried on for the tavern. Thoughts of Krampus dogged him. Who else in the village would the monster want? Having no illusions about his rectitude, he figured he was the prime candidate. Stories of his cruelty and meanness abounded. A substitute was what he needed. He had intended to employ Hans and Helga as caroling distractions while he snatched a few of the schneeballens old woman Heidrich made each year for Christmas. But if his father was not lying about Krampus, maybe they could serve a different purpose.

Johan stopped in front of the post office. Across the lane on the boardwalk in front of the chemist, a cat sat on its haunches, licking its paw and scrubbing its face. Johan knelt slowly to gather some snow into a ball. He packed it tight between his hands as he rose. The cat yawned and then raised its other paw to clean. Johan sent the snowball flying.

The cat crouched, conscious of Johan's sudden movement. The snowball glanced across its back, just behind its shoulders. The cat cried and dashed around the corner of the chemist's shop. Johan laughed. Not a direct hit, but close enough. Much of the snowball smacked against the chemist's door and stuck there, like the reverse of a bullet hole. Johan liked leaving a mark.

When he opened the door of the tavern, a warm wind hazy with pipe smoke and smelling of sauerkraut and beer swept past him into the cold night. Young men sat hunched at the four tables. A few were stuffing kraut and sausage into their mouths. Saliva ran over Johan's tongue. All were drinking beer and wiping away the froth caught in their whiskers after each gulp. This was how the unmarried men of the village spent their evenings. Johan noticed that their drinking was very different from his father's. Company or laughter never leavened his father's drunkenness.

"Close the door, you daft sod." The man cursing him sat at the nearest table. The two stared at each other.

Johan's instinct was to bloody the man's nose, but he thought better of it when he considered the heft of the man's shoulders and the size of his friends. He committed the man's face to memory. Johan's revenge could be patient.

Johan pulled the door shut. He walked toward the bar. The floorboards gave with each step and he was certain they creaked but he could hear nothing over the talk and laughter. A fire roared in the hearth. Candles burned in sconces along the walls. More candles burned on the mantle.

A young woman leaned against the bar. He had never seen her here before. The barmaid he usually dealt with was fatter and older with crow's feet at the corners of her eyes. This woman wore a dark skirt and her bodice fit tightly around her waist and chest. The sleeves of her white blouse left her shoulders bare. A scarf tied behind her neck held back her blonde locks. Her half-closed eyes suggested boredom and fatigue.

She looked him up and down. When a flicker of recognition lit her eyes, she grimaced. Somebody's sister, he thought. To have a reputation among adults, people he did not know, gave Johan a sense of pride.

"What do you want?" she said.

Remembering his father's instructions, he said, "I need to talk to Heinrich. Only to Heinrich."

She nodded toward the far end of the bar where a man with short-cropped gray hair and a trimmed gray beard spoke quietly to two older men. Johan recognized one of the two as the blacksmith.

"Question is," she said with a sneer. "Will he talk to you?"

"Of course he will. I've got coin."

When he had covered half the distance to Heinrich, Johan looked over his shoulder. The barmaid stared after him, slack jawed and incredulous.

Heinrich gestured toward the barmaid. "Tell her what you want, boy. I'm busy."

Johan pulled the silver coin from his pocket and slapped it on the bar in front of Heinrich. He did not like being dismissed.

"My father wants two bottles of schnapps."

Heinrich studied him. His expression unreadable. The other two men frowned at Johan.

"It's the stonemason's boy," said the blacksmith. "Come to beg drink for his father. Pathetic."

"Who are you calling pathetic?" said Johan.

The blacksmith studied Johan, his green eyes as sharp as the knives he hammered into being. His sandy-brown hair had nary a gray strand but a murder of crow's feet wrinkled the skin around his eyes. A scar beginning high on his cheek disappeared into his beard. He held his tankard halfway to his mouth, and Johan suspected the man's meaty hands possessed the strength to crush it.

"Too drunk to stumble here himself? Yes, I call that pathetic."

Johan clenched his fists. He agreed with the man and he was angry at his father for sending him but he couldn't abide such an insult, for the sake of his own respect.

"Borg, leave the boy alone," said Heinrich. "I'll not have blood and teeth spilled here."

The blacksmith grunted and then filled his mouth with beer.

"So you're the stonemason's boy?" said Heinrich.

Johan nodded.

Heinrich grinned. "You should have said so."

Johan shrugged.

Heinrich examined the coin and then rubbed it between his fingers. He leaned toward Johan and whispered in a breath laced with garlic. "Go around to the back door."

Johan held out his hand. "I need my coin back. The coin for the schnapps."

"My coin," said Heinrich. "Now go around or you'll get nothing."

Johan was not the trusting sort, but maybe this was how it was to work now. "Very well. I'll meet you round back."

Heinrich grinned and nodded.

Johan walked past the barmaid and her bare shoulders, past the young men gathered in camaraderie. He hated all of them.

He tromped around the front of the tavern, where the curtains were drawn across the window. Beggars got scraps of food at the back, not paying customers. Maybe the gendarme had forbidden the tavern from selling to his father but Heinrich had no scruples. He shook his head and hissed through his teeth. His anger drove away any fear of passing through the dark, close alleyway.

After he rounded the back of the tavern, he waited in front of the door, expecting it to open momentarily. Five yards behind him stood a grove of pines and beyond the pines, the slope rose sharply at the base of the Three Sisters. Johan watched the door. He stepped forward and hammered it with his fist. He listened for footsteps inside. As still as the grave. Johan hammered again in bewildered frustration. Did Heinrich think he would return empty-handed for the thrashing of his life? A branch snapped. Johan whirled around.

The moonlight didn't penetrate beyond the first few trees. He peered into the darkness. Anything could have snapped a branch, he thought, a badger, a fox? Maybe Heinrich planned an ambush, but to what purpose? He had his coin already. Wind whispered through the pines, bending their tops.

The hairs on the back of his neck rose. He felt something watching him. He felt its gaze touching him. Pine needles rustled as if crushed under foot. Johan sought the source, listening intently.

Two dots of yellow glided behind the trees, appearing and disappearing. Needles rustled in their wake. A wolf? Gooseflesh prickled his arms. He felt an urge to run. If the eyes had come toward him, he would have fled down the alleyway in a heartbeat, damn the schnapps and the thrashing from his father.

The eyes stopped. Johan's gaze met the creature's. Terror rooted him. He felt his mind delved, like a worm twisting through his thoughts, testing connections, tasting memories. Whatever watched him meditated evil against him. The malevolence engulfed him like a fog and condensed on his skin, bathing him in his own demise. Droplets gathered to join larger droplets, building momentum. Johan gritted his teeth. The veins in his neck stood out, but he could not wrest his gaze from the amber eyes. And then they disappeared.

The malevolence lingered, a weight like shackles around his ankles. The night wind pricked his skin with needles of ice. He had been sweating.

"Nothing there but trees."

Johan jumped at the sound of the voice behind him. Heinrich stood in the doorway, a bottle of schnapps held by the neck in each hand.

"I expect you're not afraid of the dark."

"Of course not. There was a beast among the trees."

Heinrich grunted. "Here." He held out the bottles. "Now off with you. As far and as fast as you can go. Your father's marked you as a bad apple. Not far from the tree they say."

Johan took the bottles. "Shall my father go elsewhere?"

"Of course not." Heinrich bolted the door against further talk.

The weight of the bottles tugged at his arms and he heard the drink sloshing inside. He cast a worried glance at the woods and then hurried through the alleyway to the lane. He longed for the comfort of his bed. He felt safe under the covers, with the ladder pulled up. A fox trotted across his path. He left it unmolested.

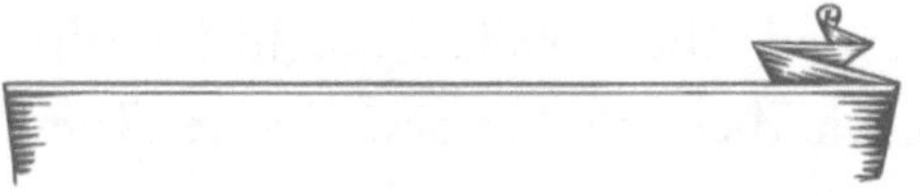

# Chapter Two
# Three Days to Christmas

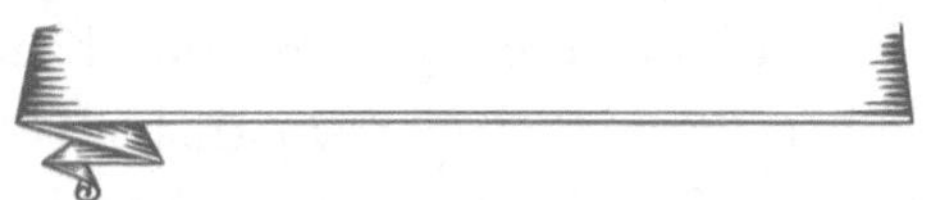

"Hans. Will you and Helga sled today?" Gunther spoke in a husky whisper. His pale-green eyes yearned with hope.

Chalk in the hands of Father Mueller scratched across the blackboard, leaving flurries of chalk dust in its wake to drift on the floor. Hans studied the boy in the neighboring row of school desks connected one to the other like the cars in a train. Gunther was an orphan before his first birthday. An avalanche buried his parents in a frozen tomb. Whispers of miracle had attended the boy's rescue. Three nuns took him in, succumbing without a fight to the call of motherhood that their profession denied them. The nuns gave Gunther as much love and moral instruction as Johan's father gave his son hatred and fear.

A dark brown birthmark the width of a finger stretched across Gunter's forehead above his left eye. Some called Gunther Scarface. Hans no longer noticed the mark. He liked Gunther. He had no reason not to.

"My father says we have to go home after school. No tarrying or we'll suffer the switch."

"What sin did you commit?"

Hans grinned. The nuns had taught Gunther to weigh all wrongdoing on the scales of sin. "None. There's rumors of Krampus."

Though he whispered, the name Krampus drew the startled attention of neighboring children. Behind each pair of wide eyes, Hans imagined the owners calculating their relative goodness as he had done the night previous. Krampus might visit a village once during a villager's youth, but every year they heard the tales from far-off villages of naughty children beaten with birch rods or snatched and eaten.

"We'll have little to fear," said Gunther.

"Livestock's gone missing, and the tracks were goat hooves."

"Goat hooves," said Gunther. "The evil one."

Hans felt the weight of someone's stare. Johan sat two seats behind Gunther. The bully looked comical squeezed into the desk. His father could have used the lad's help with the stonework, but rumor said Johan's father was never sober enough to file the paperwork so Johan remained an oversized schoolboy, much to everyone's detriment. Hans met his tormentor's gaze. The lump on his head pulsed with pain.

Johan's tongue twisted around inside his mouth and his jaws churned as he chewed on something. Johan winked. Hans thumbed his nose at him.

Gunther twisted around in his seat. Johan greeted him with a rude gesture.

Without acknowledging the insult, Gunther turned back to Hans. "You'll only invite more trouble."

Gunther refused to rise to Johan's baiting. The nuns had instilled a remarkable strength of will in the boy. If Hans were honest with himself, he envied Gunther's resistance and found it annoying as it put Hans's weakness in stark relief.

"You don't know the half of it," said Hans.

"Quiet!" Father Mueller's command bounced off the back wall of the school room. The man was as squat as he was wide, his arms as thick as his legs. His bald head glowed with the warmth of a polished brass knob. In his former life, Father Mueller had been an infantry sergeant. He may have swapped his stripes for a collar, but his methods of molding the young for battle, albeit this one spiritual, had changed little. Endless drill.

The priest snatched up a yard-long wooden rod which served to point and correct. He tapped the first line of the catechism written across the blackboard.

"In unison. Now!"

The students recited the words with the enthusiasm of an exhausted dray horse.

"Again." His voice cut with a two-edged sword of frustration and determination. With the pointer, he rapped each syllable against his desk. The sentence took on the rhythm of soldiers loading muskets.

"You must feel the words." Father Mueller tapped his chest. "In here. You must carve them into your heart to understand their power and to live them."

Hans considered the priest's admonition. Father Mueller's instructions always sounded physically painful.

He spoke the next line of the catechism as he wrote it, drawing out the syllables to match the speed of his voice to his hand. The folds of flesh at the back of his neck tightened and relaxed with the rhythm of his exaggerated speech.

A white spot appeared on the back of Father Mueller's black cassock between his shoulder blades. A titter rippled across the school room. If he heard the giggles, the priest ignored them. Hans peered at the spot, which glistened wet and sticky, a spit wad. Hans thought of Johan working his tongue and teeth.

Splat! The next wad stuck to the back of Father Mueller's bald head above the rolls of muscled flesh. The priest dropped his chalk. Giggles erupted across the schoolroom. Father Mueller slapped the back of his head with an audible thwack as if he meant to crush a mosquito.

The schoolroom fell silent as the class held its collective breath, wondering if the punishment would be corporate or individual. The stick of chalk had cracked in two at Mueller's feet. Rrrh. Rrrh. Rrrh. One piece rolled across the wooden floor, stopping against the leg of the priest's desk.

Hans turned to look down the neighboring row of desks in time to see Johan toss a rolled sheet of paper beneath Gunther's bench. Johan winked. Hans faced forward, determined to ignore the over-sized imp who called himself a man-to-be, but the derisive wink stuck in his memory and refused to disappear. Johan's glare licked the back of Hans's neck, as hot and wet as the spit wad on Father Mueller's head.

The priest rubbed his hand across the back of his head and then examined his palm. He faced the class, pinching the wad between thumb and forefinger.

"Who did this?" Father Mueller's gaze swept the class. The vengeful lord of the Old Testament fired his eyes.

No one spoke against Johan. Hans was certain someone else had seen him. They all knew Johan would visit tenfold the punishment on the tattler as Father Mueller would inflict on Johan. If he accused Johan, Hans knew he would never see the presents again.

"I demand to know!" Father Mueller slapped his pointer across the desk. Those who didn't jump at the mighty thwack, flinched. Hans imagined the slender field of sharp pain that rod would leave across his backside. The former sergeant's arms rivaled the thickness of his father's.

"Cowards!" said Father Mueller. "Are you afraid? To fear evil is to abet it. To hide from your enemy is to run from him. Did the holy martyrs shrink from their persecutors?"

Hans twisted on his bench. He gripped the edge of his desk, turning his knuckles white. The holy martyrs died. Their deaths were not quick or painless. He bowed his head. He dared not look up and find the priest's gaze locked on him. His conscience called him to speak, but the flesh that remembered Johan's boot crushing his chest counseled patience. He pressed his feet into the floor, willing his reluctant legs to stand.

"Gunther did it."

The deep voice came from behind him. Hans turned to see Johan standing, the center of the students' attention.

"I saw him," said Johan. "Look under his desk."

Father Mueller stepped toward Gunther's desk. Disappointment creased his forehead. His brows crowded together, narrowing his eyes.

Gunther shook his head, withering like a summer puddle under the hot fury of Father Mueller's glare.

The priest reached beneath Gunther's desk to retrieve a rolled sheet of paper. He unrolled it as he stood. A corner of the page was missing, the tear jagged. The side facing Hans crawled with small print, but he discerned thick, black type visible through the paper like the lettering on a title page.

Father Mueller scowled. "Gunther, take out your reader and open it."

Gunther shook his head. "I would never rip a page from a book, Father."

Hans knew that to be true. The nuns revered their books and taught Gunther no less. He felt a sense of relief wrap him like a well-worn blanket. This test would exonerate the boy, freeing Hans of any need to testify. He peered at Johan, who continued to stand, chest out, hands behind his back. The muscles in his arms stretched the fabric of his shirt. He grinned wickedly and again winked at Hans.

Gunther placed his reader on his desk. He bit his lower lip as he studied the cover. His face was flushed. Hans thought the skin glistened like the sheen of water on melting ice.

Father Mueller sighed. His hand shot forward and flicked back the cover. The heavy paperboard struck the worn wood of the desktop with a thump of finality.

The children who could see the book gasped as one. Gunther stared at the table of contents. No one breathed or spoke. Gunther closed his mouth and swallowed. Hans heard the muscles in Gunther's throat clinch together to force down his saliva.

"I didn't do it, Father. I didn't."

"The first step on the road to redemption is confession." Father Mueller spoke with a controlled voice, but his face burned red, evidence of the rage boiling below the surface, like the steaming pools at the hot springs. Hans feared for Gunther.

The explosion would drive the cane. "Do you know why we confess?"

"To accept responsibility and begin the process of cleansing our souls."

Hans watched Johan. The bully was grinning at the drama between Mueller and Gunther. When he noticed Hans, he narrowed his eyes and shook his head. His grin flattened to a scowl.

"Very good." Father Mueller looked at the grandfather clock against the far wall. A half hour remained in the school day.

"You may all leave early today. Gunther will stay."

Father Mueller stood before his desk and dismissed each row in turn. As Hans passed the door, he saw Gunther sitting with his head bowed.

The children pushed to squeeze two and three through the door, exchanging heat for the cold wind and snow of the schoolyard. They donned their hats and mittens as they stumbled outside as if they feared Father Mueller would call them back at any moment. Once outside, they were beyond his reach.

The cold bit the exposed skin of Hans's face, sharpening his senses. The smothering warmth of the over-heated classroom had dulled his thinking.

"Gunther would never do such a thing," said Helga.

"It was Johan," said Hans. "I saw him chewing the paper."

"Why didn't you say something?"

"Our favor to Johan. Remember?"

"I'm going back. Gunther's our friend."

"It's too late." Hans grabbed Helga's arm.

"Let go of me." Helga hit Hans in the chest with her free hand. Frustration rather than anger powered her arm. Hans's fingers curled in a tight grip around the loose material of Helga's sleeve. The girl wasn't going anywhere.

"Told you I'd get us out of school early and that bootlicker Gunther is paying for it." Johan laughed along with the two boys with him.

"I saw you," said Hans.

Johan stopped laughing. He faced Hans. His brows were pressed together, his eyes questioning. "And?"

A gust of wind drove fine pellets of snow from a neighboring drift. The flecks of ice peppered their faces and crackled against the frozen, hard-packed ground. Hans was like the snow pellets to Johan's ice, annoying but impotent to wreck real damage. He pushed ahead.

"The debt's paid."

Hans didn't see Johan's hand until it connected with his shoulder. He stumbled backward and without the support of Helga—he had not let loose her coat—would have fallen.

Johan gripped Hans's collar and lifted the boy onto his toes.

Hit him, thought Hans. Why isn't Helga beating him? He's the tormentor.

"I've got something you want." Johan's hot breath, stained with sausage and onions, blasted Hans's face. "I tell you what it's worth when I'm good and ready." Johan shook him.

Hans held onto his sister for balance. He felt the combined weight of the children in the schoolyard staring. No one came to his aid.

"I didn't say what I saw."

"No one did. Poor Gunther. He can count his real friends today, on no hands." Johan turned his back on Hans. The stonemason's son walked away, the confrontation finished.

More pellets peppered Hans's face, bringing tears to his eyes.

"Go home." Hans pushed Helga toward their farm.

"Where are you going? Father said—"

"Go. Home," he hissed over his shoulder. "I'll be back later." Hans stalked toward the trail up the Three Sisters.

KRAMPUS SAT CROSS-LEGGED on the floor of a cave. The short and narrow entrance—hardly wider than one man abreast—gave some cover from the wind, but on a mountainside in winter, the wind was always relentless in its effort to quash any warmth that defied it. The wind had indeed found Krampus. It whistled at him, tossed snow into the cave, and sent icy breathes into every crevice to suck the warmth out of any living thing.

Krampus barked and laughed at the wind. He waggled his long tongue to catch errant snowflakes swirling round his head. He smacked his lips. Snow tasted good. As a creature of winter, cold did not trouble Krampus. The summer sun brought agony to his long-haired hide, so he spent the warmer months hibernating in caves accessed through deep glacial crevasses.

He swiped his tongue at a floating flake. When it didn't melt, he cursed and tried to spit it out. The flake was a downy, white chicken feather. Krampus hated the taste of feathers. This one adhered to his rough tongue like lichen to a rock.

He stuck his snake of a tongue out as far as it would go, well over a foot. The pointed tip wriggled like a worm on a hook. Slowly, he drew his tongue into his mouth, scraping the rough top with his teeth. The errant feather caught on his upper lip. He spat it aside. The wind caught it, whisked it round in a spiral, and then dropped it. The feather floated to the floor, where it joined a pile of brown and white feathers blanketing Krampus's crossed hooves.

At the back of the cave, a white duck paced to-and-fro inside a makeshift cage of larch branches lashed tight with yarn twisted from Krampus's own hair. The duck quacked.

Krampus snarled in return.

The duck shook its clipped wings. It loosed a torrent of quacks as it ran from one side of its prison to the other.

Krampus laughed. Inspiring terror amused him. It was his calling.

He rotated the spit over the fire a quarter turn. Feathers stuck to the thick, blonde, wiry hair covering his arms and the back of his hands. Grease dripped from the roasting chicken and sizzled in the heart of the fire. The fiend drew a deep breath through his nose, reveling in the aroma of roasting meat. The flames leapt to attention, reaching for the chicken to lick more. The fire shared his rapacious hunger.

Krampus jabbed at the breast. The skin had become crisp and crackled when his claw cut through it to the moist meat inside. His mouth watered at the sound. Blood and grease bubbled out of the cut. Krampus's tongue shot from his mouth to lick the juices.

"Mmmmm," hummed Krampus. "Yum, yum." Chicken was good, and duck was better, and piglets were the best, but nothing was as good as plump children. Why did Christmas come only once a year? Why not celebrate the Thirteen Nights of Krampus with the mother of all glutinous feasts on the final night?

Krampus plucked more feathers and watched them float down to the pile on his lap. The fire drew some of them to itself, where the errant feathers swirled in the fire's breath before blackening to ash. The fire did not reach out for more feathers the way it did for grease, so Krampus assumed the fire cared for them as little as he did.

Why were birds covered in feathers? He once roasted a chicken without plucking the feathers, thinking they would burn away, but the result was a blackened mess, unfit to eat. It had smelled bad, too. He had thrown the carcass outside, where wolves attracted by the smells of meat fought over it.

He plucked the last feathers from the chicken. It joined the already roasting bird on the spit. Saliva dribbled across his lips and then dripped onto his lap. Done with the plucking, he brushed the pile of feathers off his legs with one great sweep of his arms. The wind caught many of them. They rose and swirled like a blinding snow squall. Others found a quick death in the fire or stuck in the floor's gritty detritus of bones and ash.

Krampus leapt to his hooves. He roared at the swirling feathers. He swatted at them with claw-tipped hands, driving them toward the cave entrance. He trotted from one side of the cave to the other, front to back, chasing feathers as a dog chases errant sheep. Plucking feathers had tried his patience.

Between the outward draft of the wind and the inward draft of the fire, the feathers dissipated. Satisfied with his herding efforts, Krampus plopped down beside the fire.

The duck eyed him. The bird was still and quiet as a stone. The cock of its head, sideways and back, expressed concerned bewilderment. The thought pleased Krampus. He liked his quarries off balance.

With a burst of quickness that surprised even Krampus, he leapt to his hooves and pounced beside the cage where he crouched eye level with the duck, his forehead pressed against the wooden bars. His shadow enveloped the fowl, an immense black veil cast over its future. The duck waddled backward until its tail met the back wall of the cave. Krampus sniffed the sweet, frantic scent of fear. Nothing teased his nose to such delight as a garden of fear.

The duck quacked.

Krampus's tongue shot into the cage. The red, wriggling tip licked the duck where the base of its lower bill met its neck, a crisp line of orange and white. Krampus snapped his tongue back into his mouth before the duck could bite. A nasty little girl had bitten his tongue once. Krampus still winced at the memory. Forcing the little imp to watch her own tongue roast and sizzle had quelled the pain a little, but he had no interest in repeating the ordeal. The duck's fear now filled his mouth and he relished the taste.

The duck squawked. It ran around its cage in a frantic display of absolute panic, crashing its breast into the bars and biting them between its bills.

Krampus barked with laughter.

He crawled back to his seat beside the fire. He turned the spit a quarter turn. The first chicken was crisp to perfection. He couldn't wait for Christmas. Saint Nicholas had promised him a plump and very nastily behaved boy. Maybe he had already seen him in the village.

He rummaged in his rucksack for the letter. He often wondered how Good Ole Nick found his lair, for he changed it every year, but each winter when he woke from his hibernation, a letter awaited him at the mouth of his cave. He fumbled with the envelope which was stiff with a thick coating of wax to protect the contents from moisture. The letter was written on three pieces of velum stitched together with red yarn to fold and fit neatly inside the envelope.

Krampus unfolded the velum to read the large script aloud.

Dear Krampus,

Take your hide to the village of Dresden. The village of Dresden. Below a mountain with three peaks called the Three Sisters.

You may take Johan, the son of the stonemason. He is a big, nasty bully beyond help. May be dangerous.

You may take Johan. The name of the boy is Johan, son of the stonemason.

Regards,

Saint Nicholas

Merry Christmas

Good Ole Nick had scratched the name Johan in red ink. The remainder of the words were in black. Krampus read the letter again, silently this time, wrapping his lips around each syllable.

The duck quacked, breaking the thin tether holding Krampus to his concentration.

The fiend snarled, culminating the growl with a snap of his jaws. The duck backed into the far corner of its cage where it hid its neck in its feathers.

Did big mean plump, Krampus wondered? He hoped the boy had a good layer of fat on him. Crispy and juicy. Crispy and juicy. Saliva dripped from his lips to splatter on the velum. He flung the letter at his rucksack. Paying no heed to the flames, he leaned across the fire to remove the first chicken from the spit. "Crispy, juicy, crispy, juicy," he repeated. The outer layer of the chicken crackled beneath his teeth. He sucked at the grease and blood welling from the wound. The chicken was crispy and juicy.

He tore chunks of hot meat from the roasted bird in a frenzy of slashing and chewing. The larger bones he spat into the fire. He crunched the smaller ones along with the meat.

When the bird was gone, all too soon, he rested against the cave wall. He wrapped his long tongue around each finger in turn to lick it clean. He dreamed of Johan, imagining a plump boy roasting over the fire, not a scrawny chicken.

The crunch of snow underfoot ended his reverie. He scampered to the cave entrance. His nose worked the wind. Human stink. Another crunch.

HELGA STOPPED WALKING at the edge of the village, where the path through the valley snaked between thick stands of spruce and pine before climbing to alpine meadows. Jagged gray peaks capped with snow defined the wide valley, embracing it with unforgiving rock. Soon after reaching the meadows a trail left the main path and led across hills of smooth snow to her parent's farm.

The snow around her sparkled in the afternoon sun. The brightness rendered the shadows beneath the trees deeper. The brightest day and the darkest night stood side by side. She hesitated to plunge into the sweet green scent of the spruce and the amber sap tang of the pines.

Gunther was innocent. The crack of the switch snapped in her thoughts. Hans was wrong. The gifts did not matter.

Helga turned about. She fought through slush softened by a day of sun, boots, hooves, and sled runners. The watery mix of snow and ice slurped at her boots. She could taste the warm scents of sausage and yeast bread wafting between the shops, but she ignored them and plunged ahead for the school. She might be in time to stay the switch.

Father Mueller liked to talk before he punished. He sought confession and contrition. Gunther would suffer more strokes if he refused to confess.

Helga's breathes clouded in front of her in puffs of white condensation. She found the schoolyard empty, nary a pupil in sight. The door gave way without resistance. She hurried down the hall lined with tarnished brass hooks where the children hung their coats, hats, and scarves. Only one hook was occupied. Her wet boots slapped the wooden planks which answered her passing with squeaks and groans.

She arrived at the threshold of the classroom to hear a thwack followed by a stifled cry of pain. She hesitated.

"Four." Gunther's voice squeaked with wincing.

"Accept the pain, my child. Don't fight it," said Father Mueller. "Punishment is cleansing."

The switch whistled on its way to landing another thwack. Helga flinched. Her nerves had taken a hit as sure as Gunther's backside.

"Five," the boy squeaked.

"To mock your elders is an affront to God."

"No!" Helga stepped past the threshold as she spoke. The timing of her exclamation could not have been worse.

Gunther leaned over the master's desk, gripping the edge. Tears streaked his face. More puddled on the desk between his hands.

Father Mueller let the tip of the switch strike the floor with a clack. Chalk dust smudged the rod above the priest's hand and some of the white powder shook loose to drift toward the floor. His mouth hung open, bewildered at the unprecedented interruption. For once Helga did not see the neat, blonde beard surrounding Father Mueller's mouth as a symbol of fierce discipline but a vain decoration.

"Helga." He blinked, but the soldier in his bones did not wallow in surprise for long. His open mouth wrinkled into a frown and his beard bristled like an angry dog's hackles. "No, you say? You know what is not an affront to God?"

"No, Father. I— Gunther didn't do it."

Gunther caught her gaze. He mouthed no as he shook his head.

"Ah. It is very kind of you to express pity for the sinner, but to bare false witness in defense is a sin itself."

"I'm not lying, Father. Johan did it."

"Did you see Johan do this?"

"No."

"Uh-hmm. Rumors. Young Gunther has confessed and accepted his punishment. The matter of guilt is closed."

"But—"

"Are you saying he is a liar?"

Her arguments were taking her nowhere good. Gunther again shook his head in the negative.

"No. I must have been mistaken."

"Good. Now, if you will wait outside. I do not punish as public spectacle but as personal instruction. Go on. Off with you." He flicked his fingers in her direction, dismissing her.

"Yes, Father." She turned her back on Gunther, as resigned to her defeat as the boy to his undeserved punishment.

Another blow landed before her shadow left the classroom. The switch sang a higher pitch. The thwack sounded no louder but Gunther yelped before giving his count. She had not saved him, but lengthened his ordeal. She gave Father Mueller reason for anger.

Helga waited beside the hook holding Gunther's coat, sitting on a worn bench with rounded edges. Gunther counted to ten.

Father Mueller lectured more on crime, punishment, and redemption before he dismissed Gunther.

Helga stood when Gunther stepped into the hall.

The boy stopped to look at her and then allowed his gaze to drift to the floor. He sniffed back tears and snot, wiped the back of his hand across his nose. Without looking up, he trudged toward his coat.

"Why are you still here?" Gunther said.

"I thought you might need some company."

Gunther grunted. An affirmative or negative, Helga could not determine.

He donned his coat and stocking cap. Saying nothing more, he made for the door. Helga noticed the stiffness in his walk. She followed.

Outside, they crossed the schoolyard in silence. Gunther wouldn't meet her gaze nor did he try to move away from her.

"I don't know what to tell Sister Ingrid."

"Tell her the truth," said Helga.

"And admit I lied to Father Mueller?"

"Oh. Hans knows you didn't do it, but he's afraid of Johan."

Gunther regarded her with sad eyes and nodded. What more could one expect, he seemed to suggest.

"No, he's not a coward." Helga poured out the story of their encounter with Johan on the mountain.

"And why didn't you tell your parents?"

"I thought we should but Hans feared father would fight Johan's father and you know how big and angry he is."

"You're no better off than I am. Caught in a tangled weave of lies. Where is Hans?"

"I think he's up on the mountain looking for the gifts Johan took. That's the direction he tramped."

"Good luck to him. I never want to be under Johan's thumb."

Helga turned to a more cheerful tack. "You must be excited for Christmas?"

"The nuns sing and then go to mass and then sing some more." Gunther smiled as he shrugged, suggesting the situation was not as bad as it sounded.

"You could join us for Christmas. Mother wouldn't mind. How could the nuns object?"

Helga thought she had made everyone happy, unaware of her plan's black lining.

HANS'S LEG DISAPPEARED in a snow drift past his knee, compressing the fine powder with a muffled crunch. He cursed with some words he had heard his father use. Words his mother would punish him for even knowing. The swirling snowflakes dampened his harsh voice, absorbing his anger in a cloud of snow. The weather in the pass could be vastly different from the valley. A night and day of intermittent snow squalls had buried the tracks he and Helga had left the day before.

He should have been wearing snowshoes, but that would have required going home first or bringing them to school in the morning. Both courses would have drawn unwanted attention to his plans.

He extricated his leg and stepped back from the rock face to firmer ground. Snowflakes melted on his face. Fissures as jagged as bolts of lightning rived this stretch of rock in abundance. Some were no more than cracks. Others were wide and tall enough to admit a man. Hans was certain Johan had secreted the gifts in one of the larger crevices.

The rock face rose hundreds of feet above him and disappeared into the snow clouds. Fingertips of black, white, and quartz speckled the gray rock. From the failing light, he guessed an hour separated him from sunset. If he arrived home before dark he wouldn't be in so much trouble. He hoped. Check a couple more fissures, he decided.

Passing around an outcrop, Hans stopped in his tracks. He sniffed. Smoke, definitely a fire, but roasting chicken? Hunger squeezed his stomach as his mouth filled with saliva. He sniffed more, trying to locate the direction of the warm, succulent scent of roasting meat. The winds whorled around the peaks in circular patterns, seeming to blow in every direction at once. The cook fire had to be close. He could taste the fat dripping into the fire.

Hans crept forward along the rock face. He cursed the snow crunching with each step and gripping at his boots. Anyone listening would hear him coming. Helga would say they should fetch the gendarme or Father Mueller or some other adult. It was true. No one living rough at this time of year could be up to good, but Hans had trouble believing his nose. He needed confirmation from his eyes.

The scent grew stronger. He passed a couple fissures that warranted searching but pressed ahead, following his nose. All thoughts of the stolen gifts forgotten.

He passed another outcrop and spied his quarry. The narrow mouth of a cave glowed with firelight, flickering bright and dim in response to the fire's dance. The scents of smoke and cooking filled his nose as well as a peculiar musky scent that he likened to a goat but not quite. Someone might use a goat as a beast of burden, he decided.

Hans crunched toward the entrance, cursing the snow for screaming his approach. He also angled away from the rock, thinking to peer inside from a distance. A head start in a chase was never a disadvantage.

No one.

Hans was mystified. There was a well-tended fire and a chicken on a spit. He looked left, right, and behind, wondering if the occupant had heard his approach and was now hiding. Maybe watching him.

"Hello? Anyone here?"

Quack.

A duck? The call came from the cave. He looked in every direction, nothing but snow, rock, and trees. The spruce and larch worried him. Johan had secluded himself in the shadows below the branches. Hans crept toward the cave.

"Hello?"

Quack.

He remembered his father saying that chickens and ducks had been stolen. And a dog's head had been bashed in.

The fire crackled and popped, orange and red, as it ate through wood. Dead branches broken into foot-long faggots were heaped nearby ready to feed the flames. The ends were jagged. Snapped, not chopped with an ax.

The heat rising from the entrance carried smoke into his eyes. He crouched a foot from the entrance. The cave was barely wider than a man at its entrance and tapered into the mountain no more than ten feet. The roasting chicken was still raw. Feathers blanketed the floor.

Quack.

Peering into the farthest reaches, he spied the waddling movement of something white. The duck.

When Hans stood, he noticed the tracks. Hoof prints in the snow leading away from the cave. He swallowed as his mouth went dry. His heart leapt to a sprint, goaded with birch rods of fear.

He struggled to muster the courage to move his stiffening legs. With a burst of determination he squeezed inside the cave and grabbed the duck from its cage. The inside of the cave was warm with the fire, but terror threatened to freeze him more than the cold. Krampus was waiting outside. Why had he risked his life to save a duck, already destined for someone's table? He bolted sideways out the entrance. No Krampus.

With the quacking duck wedged under his arm, Hans ran for the village, sometimes flying several strides down the slope. He couldn't keep this discovery a secret, no matter how much trouble he would bring down on himself.

KRAMPUS STOOD IN THE dark inside his ruined cave. Moonlight reflected off the snow outside, casting a silver glow over chicken bones and downy white feathers trampled into the cave-floor grit. The faint scent of roasting fowl lingered though the stink of men nearly overpowered it. The ashes and faggots for his fire had been scattered. The duck he had looted from a careless farmer had been stolen. All his plans upended.

He could no longer live here. It would take a season to air out the stink and he couldn't risk them coming back. He kicked at feathers, bones, and sticks, lifting them with his hooves and sending them clattering against the walls.

He stepped outside onto the snow stamped with boot prints. His lumpy bag hung over his shoulder down his hairy back. He should scout the village to find the whereabouts of this miscreant Johan and his stonecutter father, but not tonight.

Krampus barked at the moon and yowled. Somewhere a child heard the call and burrowed its head beneath its pillow in a fear as instinctual as eating. Krampus laughed. He once came upon a pack of wolves howling at the moon. When he loosed his cry, the beasts had scattered to the four winds, yelping as if he'd struck them.

No, tonight he would find a new cave. Why Good Ole Nick didn't let him tag along, Krampus didn't understand. Nick could point out the offending child's home and save Krampus a lot of bother. But Saint Nick had his rules and the old coot was a stickler for them.

With the moon at his back, Krampus stalked higher up the mountain. If there was one thing he excelled at, it was finding a hole in the ground.

# Chapter Three
# Two Days to Christmas

In the yard outside the school, where the fresh snow had been stomped to slush, Hans was the center of attention, a veritable hero, a warrior child who had frightened Krampus away. His schoolmates crowded around to hear his tale. Their collective breathing shrouded him in a cold, white mist.

Hans did his best to heighten the danger he felt when approaching the fiend's lair. The snow crunched, the fire crackled, and the beast grunted. Hans's heart clawed at his ribs. His body burned with fear. Snowflakes melted before they touched him. But he soldiered ahead, drawing strength from the danger. Gunther likened the encounter to St. George slaying a dragon. All believed Hans had banished Krampus from their village for the season.

Johan stood alone, leaning against the schoolhouse, scowling from far outside the circle of Hans's admirers.

The story Hans told was not all fiction and exaggeration. The boy had acted with honor. After braving the cave to rescue the duck from a makeshift cage of larch sticks, he had found the gendarme to report his find. The gendarme gathered some men and bade Hans to lead them back up the mountain. The gendarme accompanied Hans home to explain to Hans's father and mother what a great service the boy had done for the village.

Hans's father praised his son's bravery. He praised Hans for following the noble path—rescuing the stolen duck and summoning the gendarme. Then he beat Hans for disobeying and banished the boy to bed without supper. A good lesson. Hans remembered it for all the rest of his days.

The praise of his peers in the cold schoolyard lessoned the sting of his father's wrath before the family hearth. Despite overcoming the danger on the mountain and suffering a beating, he hadn't found the gifts. He now suspected Johan had stashed them near at hand. Perhaps Johan secreted them under his bed or among the rafters of his cottage.

Hans noticed Johan scowling at him from under the eve of the schoolhouse. He sneered back and stepped toward the bully. His right foot slipped sideways when he expected it to hold still. He flung his arms out for balance, saving his behind from a wet encounter.

Johan laughed. "You're as sure footed as a three-legged goat."

"You should be thanking me," said Hans.

"Thanking you? Did you bust your noggin on the mountain?" Johan grinned.

The private joke stung. "I sent Krampus packing. I'll wager you were at the top of the fiend's list."

The other schoolchildren had gathered behind Hans. Voices concurred with Hans's opinion.

Johan grabbed his gut as he guffawed. "You think mean old Krampus is quaking at the sight of a scrawny boy? He eats little boys, you idiot."

Hans paused. His retort slipped off his tongue, the words hollow and ineffectual. Johan had a point. None of Hans's friends voiced a defense.

"Well, Krampus did run away." Hans noticed a snowball arc high overhead. It glittered in the sun before landing on the roof. "The gendarme and I saw the goat hoof tracks."

"He'll find a new hole to hide in. And now he's pissed at you for taking his duck." Another snowball sailed overhead to land on the roof. Johan's gaze flicked upward for a moment to follow it. "I'd say *you're* at the top of Krampus's list."

Two snowballs flew overhead. Hans saw Gunther carefully calculating his throw.

"Missed, you idiot." Johan snarled at Gunther. "Do I need to give you lessons in hitting your target?"

Hans realized Gunther's intention. A snowdrift perched on the edge of the steep roof above where Johan stood. A few well-placed balls of slush might dislodge the drift, a mini-avalanche.

Hans wanted to play a role in Gunther's gambit. All he needed to do was distract Johan.

"Are you so good with spitballs that you can teach us?"

Johan turned his ire back on Hans. "I could teach all of you."

"Why are you goading him," whispered Helga from behind. "The gifts?"

"We're never getting them back," said Hans.

"Then we should tell—"

The snow fell without crying a warning. It smothered Johan's surprised yelp. His head and chest disappeared in a sparkling, white blanket.

Everyone behind Hans laughed, or so it sounded to him. Johan's shape emerged as snow flew in every direction, like water shaken from a dog's back. He shook his head and beat his arms against his chest to dislodge the powdery white wetness which clung to his woolen hat and coat with the grip of wet flour.

"You bastard. You orphan bastard." Johan's snarl gave him the look of an evil snow monster. He charged at the knot of school kids behind Hans, his gaze focused on Gunther.

A collective scream pierced the cold morning. Hans felt more than saw everyone run. Slush splashed underfoot only to be squished and kicked under another foot. He watched Johan charging, a beast of pure anger—all raging red eyes and gnashing teeth. The sight frightened and yet held him. He recalled his father telling him of a man who stood paralyzed with fear as a bull gored him. Hans had thought the man crazy stupid, but now he understood. His legs didn't move. His instinct to flee had deserted him. He watched the snow-coated fury closing in.

A hand gripped Hans's arm and yanked him sideways off-balance, so his legs had no choice but to follow Helga's lead.

"Johan!" Father Mueller's battle-sergeant voice commanded Johan to stop and he did.

The children had retreated to the far reaches of the schoolyard. Helga dragged Hans aside. Johan was in for a beating this day. No matter his explanation.

Johan's cold gaze flicked between Gunther and Hans. Hans read cruelty and fear in those eyes, a dangerous combination. Krampus was not the only fiend stalking the village.

JOHAN PRESSED HIS BACK to the cupboards, like a mouse squeezing into a dark corner. A knob burrowed at his shoulder blade. The knot of discomfort kept him alert. He bit into a sausage he held and chewed slowly, quietly. The tangy spices gifted a bite to the sweet, fatty meat—a delicious contrast to the sour stink of sweat, schnapps, and stale bread that stagnated in the cottage.

His father sat slumped over his elbows at the end of the table, humming a ballad off key and off tempo in between gulps of schnapps from a wooden cup. A single candle, with one end jammed down the neck of a bottle, burned at the table's center. The dim, wavering light joined the glow from the dying fire in the hearth to create shadows for Johan to hide in.

He doubted his father knew he was there or cared if he wasn't. Surprise could be dangerous depending on the old drunk's mood. A soft word might be answered with a cuff across the mouth and the coppery slick taste of blood on his lips. Johan swallowed before cutting into the sausage with his teeth.

Now was the time to speak—before the old man was drunk senseless and unable to reason a worry over the future.

Johan stepped forward, cutting the distance to the table in half while remaining out of range of those thick, cuffing paws. Scars crisscrossed Karl's knuckles and the back of his hands. The stones clawed at their cutter.

"Father?"

The humming stopped. "Eh? Is that you, boy? Quit lurking about and get over here where I can see you."

Johan moved to the opposite end of the table, well out of cuffing range. He was baiting a bear held with a chain flaking with rust.

"The tavern will be closed tomorrow. It's Christmas. Shouldn't you send me for more bottles?"

Karl cocked his head. He blinked deliberately, as if clearing his inner vision.

"Christmas? Tomorrow? No. The next day. Got it wrong, boy. Want your gift early?" He flashed his yellow teeth. His bloodshot eyes glistened. Maybe it was a joke but Johan saw a sneer.

He bit back a laugh. Other than the hat on his head, he hadn't received a gift in what? Four years? Five years?

"No. It's tomorrow. You don't want to catch yourself short on Christmas."

"No. No, can't be." He shook his head and then gulped more schnapps. The gurgle of the liquid burning down his dull throat was audible. "But—"

Johan imagined the overly greased gears turning and slipping in his father's dull head. Drowning in drink was for cowards who didn't have the guts to commit suicide.

"Tomorrow is Christmas. Father Mueller told us so at school today."

"Did he? Lying—" Karl slurred some incomprehensible and blasphemous syllables.

Johan's apprehension grew. If his plan had any hope of success, he needed his father passed out tomorrow night, not now. If he could convince his father tomorrow would be Christmas, the old drunk would drink himself into a dead stupor before supper time.

"Tomorrow *is* Christmas. You'll run out if—"

Karl smacked his fist against the table. The plates clattered. The bottle with the candle wobbled and then rolled around on its base—rrrum, rrrum, rrum, rum—before settling. "I'm thinking. Can't think with you yacking." Karl looked about, brows furrowed, as if he had lost something. "Christmas. Tomorrow. Why, that means tonight is Christmas eve."

Johan nodded. He could feel his father slipping, accepting the lie.

"You shouldn't go out tonight. Krampus will get you. He's angling for you." Karl chuckled as he shook his finger at Johan.

The old fool. Krampus was the reason for this charade.

"I'll take care."

"Aye, you'd be a bitter, choking meal." Karl extracted his coin purse. Coins clinked together on the table.

Johan felt his plan stitching together. He'd only half believed in the possibility. Despite his best efforts to hide it, a genuine smile pushed through the mud of fear and anger that suppressed any sense of joy.

Karl pushed a pile of coins at Johan. "For three bottles." His yellow teeth appeared again, poking out of his red gums.

Johan gathered up the coins, counting them, hoping for a stray coin extra, but there were none. Even drunk his father made no errors with money.

"Only Heinrich?"

Karl nodded. "I'd pay Krampus no thought. Even if he got you, I'd only be out a mouth to feed."

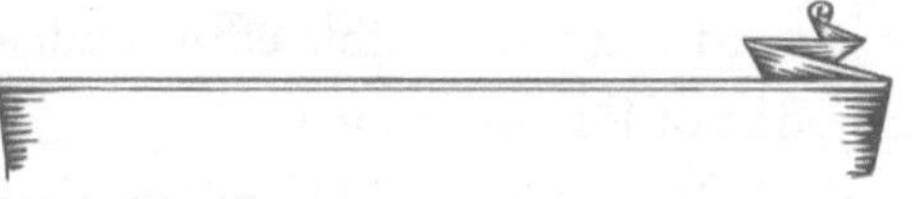

# Chapter Four
# Christmas Eve

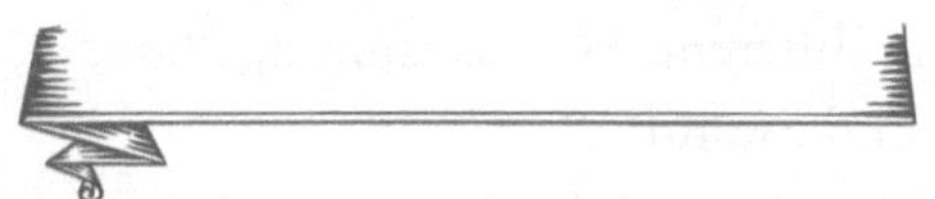

Helga stood beside Gunther in the schoolyard. Snow had fallen overnight, adding a clean layer of white that reflected the afternoon sun with the luster of innocence. She squinted against the brightness from above and below. She liked winter for the snow. It hid the ugly patches of the world under a neat layer of white. Other students streamed around them as they waited for Hans.

"How did you know the snow on the roof would fall on Johan?" said Helga. Johan had not come to school so she felt safe talking about him in the yard.

"A lucky guess." Gunther shrugged. "It looked precarious clinging to the edge of the roof."

"I thought it was very clever."

Gunther nodded. His face flushed redder than the wind warranted.

"My father has a chess and a checkers set."

"I don't know how to play chess. The nuns aren't much for games."

"No matter. I can teach you."

"Krampus is going to get you, Scarface," said a passing boy.

Gunther winced and with visible effort endeavored not to look at the boy, one of Johan's cronies.

"Look in the mirror, Martin." Helga's insult fell across the boy's back.

"It's best to ignore them," said Gunther.

"You didn't ignore Johan."

"That was different. He was taunting Hans."

"I don't understand."

"I feel right when I defend someone, but—"

"Not when you defend yourself?"

Gunther nodded. "Has your mother really baked streusel?"

"She does every Christmas. I told her you're partial to apples."

"I wish I could eat supper at your table every day." He frowned. "I mean, even now and again would be wonderful. I wouldn't want to impose."

Helga laughed. "Don't be silly. I'll talk to mother. Maybe you can come once a month or once a week. I'm certain she'll say you're too thin."

"Hans!" Gunther turned to wave.

Helga's older brother trudged toward them. He had the shellshocked look of someone who had received extremely good or bad news. And Father Mueller never kept someone late to praise them.

"What's wrong?" said Helga.

"Can't be so bad," said Gunther. "He didn't expel you."

"He wants me to do extra lessons next semester."

"All semester? Is this because of Johan?" Gunther frowned and furrowed his brows with indignation.

"No. He thinks my work is good enough to enter the cathedral school in Branstz. He gave me a letter for father and mother."

"Branstz?" said Helga. "But that's a two day journey in summer."

"Father Mueller says it's a boarding school."

"That's wonderful," said Gunther. "You'll be a scholar."

"I don't know what I think." Hans grinned. "I thought I was in for a whipping."

They left the schoolyard a laughing trio. Helga was pleased for Hans but doubts clouded the horizon. If Hans lived in Branstz for much of the year, she would never see him and she would have more chores to do.

None of them noticed the shadow lurking in the trees outside the village.

Johan leapt in front of them, growling and waving his hands with fingers bent like claws.

Helga screamed. In the dim light of the forest path, the tall and bulky Johan resembled some ill-tempered creature. The boys stumbled backward.

Johan laughed. "If I was Krampus, you three would be birch-whipped and in my bag."

"Father Mueller is looking for you." Gunther stepped forward, angling his body in front of Helga.

"Let the old windbag look."

Helga gasped. Was it a sin to speak of a priest in that manner?

"And Krampus will find one like you, Scarface. You're marked."

"Get out of our way," said Hans.

"Ha! Speaking of looking, I've got something you're looking for." Johan poked a thick index finger into Hans's chest. "Meet me outside my father's cottage after mass. If not, I'll have two more gifts to open come morning."

Johan jeered as he disappeared into the woods.

Helga turned to her brother. The questions of Branstz and boarding school seemed infinitely far away in comparison to Johan's challenge.

JOHAN WAITED IN THE shadowed alleyway between the butcher and the land surveyor. He had chased away two cats with hard-packed snowballs and several rats using a discarded length of split lumber. He enjoyed the alley to himself, for now. The quiet solitude would not last. The scavengers would return, unable to stay away. The rotting mix of assorted offal insulted his nose and his human snout was nowhere near as sensitive.

The afternoon sun had melted snow near the front edge of the roof. The dripping had formed a puddle, now a slick expanse of ice. Moonlight flashed off the watery glass. Johan studied the edges where thin layers had cracked and shifted farther from mother ice with each disturbance of the alley's entrance. He noted the location of the ice puddles. Falling on his bum wouldn't create the proper mood when he stepped out of the shadows.

A bell had called for evening mass near an hour ago. If his plan was going to bear fruit, he would know soon. If the little brats didn't come, he wouldn't go home. His father wouldn't care. The old man was slumped over the table in a stupor, his cheek and hair stuck in a drying spill of schnapps. And, Johan repeated to himself, if Krampus could not find him, Krampus could not catch him.

A nagging girl's voice sliced through the cold night. Johan grinned. They were arguing. Typical. He poked his head out of the alley. A bonfire burned in front of the church. Three figures silhouetted against the yellowish flames. One was gesticulating, adding force to her arguments.

He ducked back into the alley. Three of them? He decided the third was Scarface Gunther and cheered at the thought. That marked runt deserved any unfortunate fate he received.

The voices grew more discernible. The sister said they didn't need the gifts and something about Brantsz? What did they know about a cathedral town? The brother told his sister to hush.

When he heard their steps on the boardwalk, Johan stepped out of the alley. The three stopped. The girl did not scream. Maybe they were too startled, too afraid to act. Frightening them had been such a delicious thrill.

"I hear you don't want those gifts."

"Of course we want them," said Hans.

"Then you shouldn't talk so loud."

"We're here," said Helga. "What do you want?"

"Come." He waved for them to follow without checking to see if they complied. Furtive whispers and their footfalls thudding against sturdy planks were evidence enough. Loud peals of laughter carried from revelers around the bonfire.

Johan considered when the parents would miss them. Why had he not factored them into his plans? Perhaps Krampus came early in the evening. He shrugged. Couldn't be helped now.

When they reached the door to his cottage, he bade them be quiet.

"You don't want to wake my father. He swings his fists as hard as he swings a hammer."

Their boots whispered across the floor planks near Johan's father without loosing a single scrape or creak. The side of Karl's head rested on the table in a pool of schnapps. He snored. Sometimes a bubble formed at the corner of his mouth and grew as the snore persisted until the bubble popped.

The bubbles reminded Johan of summertime and the masses of tiny bubbles that clung to reeds at the edges of ponds. The memory of sweet flowers filled his nose, for a moment crowding out the sour scents of the cottage. What he was about to do was not a summertime act, not even a Christmastime act, but a February thing, when the cold has seeped deep into the earth and snow weighs down the forest branches. To survive, one must fight in summer and winter. Every animal knew that rule.

"The gifts are up there." Johan pointed at the loft, accessed through a trapdoor in the ceiling and a ladder.

"We have to go up and get them?" said Hans. "Is this some kind of test?"

"Not just get them, but find them. It will take all three of you, if you don't want to spend all night looking. And aren't your parents waiting?"

The three shared looks loaded with suspicion.

"Why not just give them to us?" said Hans.

"Because that wouldn't be fun for me to watch, and if you give up, that means you forfeited them and they're mine by finder's right. You ought to get looking." Johan lit a taper and held it out for any of the three to take.

Hans frowned. He snatched the taper, mounted the ladder, and climbed. Once through, he thrust down a hand to help his sister. "I can't look everywhere by myself. Come on."

Johan struggled to hold back a smile. One more to go. Hans moved Johan's bed. The legs scraped across the ceiling. Helga urged Gunther to help them.

"Your friends need you, Scarface."

"It's not a scar." Gunther mounted the ladder.

"You're marked all the same."

As soon as Gunther's boot left the ladder, Johan sprang into action. He pulled the ladder away, dropping it to the floor. His father grunted, but Johan ignored it. Tonight, brother schnapps was his friend. A rope hung from a corner of the loft entrance. Johan leapt and grasped it in his fist.

Gunther stared at him through the opening. The boy's mouth hung open and the brows above his eyes were furrowed, the picture of bewildered confusion. So different from the bright, cocky eyes that had watched the snow fall on Johan. How sweet tasted revenge. Johan laughed as his descent pulled the rope taut. Gunther's senses had yet to catch up to the doom swinging before him.

The trapdoor slammed shut.

The rope Johan held was tied to the handle which, before this evening, had been attached to the other side of the door and allowed for lifting it. Johan wound the rope around a hook he had screwed into the ceiling. He had been a busy boy while not in school.

With the trapdoor secured and no leverage for pulling it open, Hans and company were as trapped as Jonah in the leviathan's belly. Trapped until someone came hunting for them.

Johan listened to them shout and pound on the ceiling. His father snored and blew his dream bubbles. Johan propped the ladder against the wall.

He wanted Krampus to see it.

KRAMPUS SKIPPED THROUGH the spruce and pine woods. His hooves skimmed across the snow leaving a shallow trough. Half-moon gouges marked where he kicked. It was Christmas eve, his favorite night of the year.

He spied the lights of the village ahead as he descended the slope. Church bells pealed and the smokey scent of a bonfire called him. Pine needles crunched and snapped beneath the snow.

When he left the woods the loathsome human stink struck him. A slap from the clawed paw of a great brown bear would have been less cruel. Fortunately, roasting naughty children smelled delicious. His memories of the sweet, fatty grease drippings sizzling in the fire tickled his nose. The reward paid for the unpleasant hunt. If only Christmas eve came more often.

Birch rods in hand and empty canvas bag slung over his shoulder, he loped toward the village of Dresden, following a shadowy path drawn on the snow by passing clouds. Anyone noticing the tracks in the morning would think them the meanderings of an inebriated goat.

All he needed to do was find the stonecutter's cottage and beat the naughty Johan into his bag. This hunting would be so much easier if Saint Nick allowed him to accompany the gift giver through the village, but no, Krampus had to find the miscreants all on his own.

He entered the village and looked from one house to another, imagining what delicious bundles slept inside. He peered in the windows he passed, hoping to find a wakeful child whom he could frighten. Scare its little heart up its throat and into its mouth. He giggled imagining the gory image.

Krampus wove a path through the yards and cottages. He steered toward the street with the shops. The church towers anchored his trail. Supper, breakfast, brunch—all would soon be his to enjoy. He could smell Johan roasting.

HANS HIT THE TRAPDOOR with the edge of his fist. Once, twice, thrice. Out of frustration rather than any hope of damaging the wood. The door held firm. They were stuck in this stinking loft, which smelled faintly of stale schnapps and strongly of unwashed Johan.

"We need a knife," said Gunther. "Something thin to slide through the crack and cut the rope."

"Good idea," said Helga.

Hans wondered why that thought hadn't occurred to him. Only anger raced in his thoughts. Why had he not seen the trap? And why did Helga constantly praise Gunther?

"Ow!" Hans banged his head on the steeply slanted ceiling. "How does Johan stand in here?"

The three set about searching the sparse loft for a knife. There were few places to look. Johan was not rich in possessions.

Helga held the taper above her head while the two boys tore apart Johan's bed. They tossed the blanket and sheets on the floor, prodded both sides of the straw mattress, and did the same with the pillow. The lone window—an octagon no bigger than one of their heads, far too small to climb out—admitted precious little moonlight.

They found nothing in the bed. A wooden box proved as useless. Three pennies, a toy soldier, and a silver broach with a large red garnet set in a circle of smaller yellow garnets.

"That belonged to his mother," said Helga. "Or he would have sold it."

Hans paused, surprised to consider Johan had sentimental feelings. For a moment, a very brief one, he almost felt sorry for him.

Their search moved to bundles of tattered clothes in the corners. One contained a nest of mice. When they shook the clothes, the vermin tumbled onto the floor, squeaking and scattering, scurrying between the children's legs in search of other hiding places.

Hans stared at the window. "Maybe we could use some broken glass."

A thud shivered through the cottage.

"What was that?" said Helga.

"A door?" said Hans.

"Maybe Johan has come back to let us out," said Gunther.

Hans frowned. Had they been imprisoned long enough for Johan to prove his point?

"Shhh!" Hans tapped his ear with a finger.

Someone moved about below. The hairs on the back of Hans's neck stood on end. He stared wide-eyed at Helga and Gunther.

The steps were not the footfalls of boots, but hollow clops, like hooves on wood.

KRAMPUS PLACED A CHAIR beneath the trapdoor. Did anyone think a bit of rope would thwart him on his errand? Krampus thought people so stupid. He rubbed his hands together with gleeful anticipation and clacked together the claws that tipped his long fingers.

He had found the stonemason's cottage with relative ease. Dashing from one darkened alleyway to another, Krampus had worked his way through the village, avoiding the few villagers who left the bonfire early. A yard filled with stones seemed a likely home for the stonemason.

A survey through the very dirty windows revealed someone slumped over a table. He'd seen this before. Winter merriment seemed to leave people in a stupor. Inside, the place stank more than usual of people and reeked of fermented fruit. People drank such strange things. The man slumped over the table snored and blew bubbles in his slobber.

Krampus slit the rope with a claw. Easy enough. The ceiling creaked with footsteps. He bared his sharp, yellow teeth in a hungry grin. There was no need for all the scouting and planning that Saint Nick advised. He sniffed below the door. Yum. Fear. The bad children were always the most fearful on Christmas Eve.

He kicked the chair aside. With his birch rods and canvas bag tucked under his arm, he seized the ladder. Something heavy scraped across the floor above. Krampus combed the wavy hair on his chin with his claws. Hmm. Resistance. Interesting.

He rammed the ladder against the trapdoor. It rose an inch, revealing a strip of darkness, and then crashed flush with the ceiling.

Did the little rascal think the bane of bad children would give up and go away, leave without his Christmas dinner? He barked with laughter.

Puzzles. He paced in a circle, looking up at the door and tugging harder on the hair at his chin. Thinking sometimes hurt. He liked puzzles that weren't too hard. After circling deasil and withershins—one of them always worked—an idea came to him.

He positioned the ladder against the trapdoor and pushed to wedge it into place such that the rails pressed on the boards to either side of the board with the handle. The door rose no more than an inch.

Satisfied with his preparations, Krampus bent his hairy legs and then sprang upward. He gripped the handle with both hands, swung his hooves over his head, and kicked. His hooves clomped against the ceiling. A board in the trapdoor cracked.

Krampus pulled himself up until his horns scraped the ceiling and then let his weight fall. When his extended arms caught his weight, the board cracked and then split. The handle tore away. A bedpost fell through.

Krampus gathered his birch rods and bag. He scampered up the ladder, cast the bed aside, and burst through the remains of the trap door.

"Come out, come out, you fiendish child. Krampus is here." He sprang into the loft, birch rods at the ready.

A high-pitched scream stung his ears. He twisted about, sweeping his gaze along the short sidewalls and into all the dark corners. His night vision poured into every nook like hot syrup. Night and shadows gave his holly-green eyes no trouble. He smelled fear, lots of it, overpowering the stink of human habitation. His tongue washed his lips with saliva.

"What?" He stared at three children huddled against a wall—a girl between two boys. "What's this?" Perhaps Saint Nick was right about scouting. "Which one of you is Johan?"

"He's...he's not here," stuttered the bigger of the two boys.

Krampus chuckled. He shook a finger. The yellow claw danced before them but brought forth no thoughts of sugarplums.

"I've heard that one before." He crept closer as he talked, his claw moving back and forth like a mesmerist's pocket watch. "You think me a simpleton? I've been taking care of nasty children since before your great-grandparents' great-grandparents were—. Well, maybe more great-great-grandparents. A very, very long time shall we agree?"

"It's not a lie," shouted the other boy.

"He tricked us and trapped us up here."

The children seemed to shrink as they huddled closer together. Clouds of sweet fear rolled off of them like steam from a boiling pot.

Krampus could smell the crackling fat dripping into the roasting fire. He could taste it. His eyes twinkled with delicious delight.

"I know what happened," said Krampus. "Your father tied the door shut. Some stupid attempt to keep you safe. Did he think a little rope would thwart me? Then he made himself drunk. So which one of you is Johan?"

The children shook their heads.

Krampus growled—a low, slow rumble that grew in his throat to a roar. He leapt forward. Birch rods slapped the children. Not one escaped the stinging thrashes.

He rocked back on his hooves. The whimpering mass of children intertwined their arms and legs. Krampus tugged the hair on his chin.

If one of these children was the nasty Johan then the other two were perchance just as bad? Nearly as bad? Why not take all three of them and not bother with who was Johan? Save Good Ole Nick the bother of recording their nasty deeds and give Ole Krampus three nights of feasting. His tongue shot forward, wetting fangs and lips.

When it came to more feasting, Krampus needed little convincing. He would give Saint Nick an accounting when the jolly old man came around. Surely the situation required some quick thinking.

Krampus charged at the sobbing mass of child flesh with open bag and grasping hands. He was very skilled at stuffing squirming things into a bag.

HANS KICKED AND BEAT on the rough sack, anything to tear a hole. Its threads were thick and coarse and scratched his hands and face. Gunther and Helga joined him with their own struggles but they labored in the blackness of a deep pit. Krampus shifted the burden between his shoulders. The moves shook them about, for a time turning their struggles against one another. The smell of Krampus stung their noses—the worst of goat and pig and wet wool that's been left to mildew.

Their struggles came to nothing. Krampus's stride slowed and then stopped. The bag narrowed between lips of stone and then grew plump on the other side.

Hans sensed they had entered the fiend's lair. Having seen such a cave, he knew what to expect. It gave him no comfort. Sweat rolled into his eyes. The inside of the bag was hot and stuffy from their combined struggles. Hans cursed his gullibility, his stupidity for believing Johan. He didn't deserve the cathedral school. He didn't deserve to live.

"Here you are, my little nasties. Your new home. Until I'm hungry for you." Krampus cackled, trailing off to a gurgling hiss.

The three were still in the bag as that horrible laughter—like nothing they had ever heard—raked their ears. They bounced on a hard surface and rolled to a stop against another.

Hans scrambled out the gaping bag on hands and knees. Gunther and Helga came close behind, their shoulders pressing against his hips. His eyes were starved for light from the passage in the pitch black bag. The bit of moonlight that filtered into the cave through its narrow opening seemed like a bright dawn.

They were confined at the back of a narrowing cave, scarcely wide enough for the three children to sit shoulder to shoulder. The floor and walls were cold, hard, and gritty. Their color tended from dark gray to black.

A fence of branches knotted together like the bars of a metal cage stretched from wall to wall and from floor to ceiling, hemming them in. Hans recalled the duck and the chicken bones.

Krampus worked on knots to hold the door in the cage fast. His breath hissed through his teeth. His eyes glowed with a green light all their own.

"This rope is braided from my own hair." Krampus combed his fingers through strands of long, blondish hair growing thickly on his hips. "Beautiful and nye indestructible. Too bad for naughty children." His lips curled back from his teeth when he cackled.

The fiend's fur reminded Hans of goat hair.

Krampus tugged on the door. Apparently satisfied, he hopped like a toad on all fours—his hooves clacking—to a pile of sticks and kindling. He bent over the mound and through black magic or conventional means, coaxed a red glow and a thin stream of smoke from the kindling. He blew on the fledgling fire until flames caught the twigs and then the thicker sticks.

"Aah." Krampus rubbed his palms together and clicked his claws. "I'm going to fetch some faggots for a roaring fire to warm us. And all the better to roast you. Don't go away." He shook a finger at them.

The moment his hairy back squeezed through the opening, Hans and Gunther lunged at the frail-looking cage. They shook it, pushed it, and pulled it. They twisted the bars and kicked at them. Their efforts to break the branches bore no success. Each length of bar consisted of several thin branches lashed together. What appeared flimsy was quite stout.

"Untie the knots," said Hans. He and Gunther dug with their fingers at neighboring knots, hoping to open a hole in the cage.

"Work on the door, Helga!" Hans was frantic. He reasoned this was their only chance.

Helga had been huddling against the back wall whimpering. Hans's tone startled her into action. She crawled to the door and applied her much more nimble fingers to the knots Krampus had recently tied.

The hair was slick as silk, soft as linen, and cut their fingertips like steel. Drops of blood rolled down the bars. Curses of frustration and pain filled the cave as did the crackle and smoke from burning wood.

Hans eyed the fire. One burning brand was all he needed. He could burn their way out. He reached through the bars, but even wedging his shoulder through, his arm and wriggling fingers covered less than half the distance.

"It's no use," said Helga. "It's going to eat us."

"No he's not," said Hans. "We're not Johan."

Gunther pulled his bleeding fingers from his mouth. "Any other ideas?"

A clatter of branches against the stone floor drew their attention to the cave mouth.

"Busy, busy, I see."

The dancing flames played with the shadows on Krampus's red face, rendering his angular features sharp as a blade and his green eyes as vibrant as holly.

He rushed the cage. Helga screamed. Instinct drove the three to the back wall where Helga cowered in Gunther's embrace. Hans pressed the back of his head and neck against the cold stone, wishing it would swallow him like an icy-blue glacier lake.

"What's this?" The fiend played badly at surprise. Hans recognized a cunning in Krampus's eyes that spread down his face like cracks in weak ice to animate the corners of his mouth. Death and danger hid beneath that cunning. He was toying with them. A cat with a mouse, by comparison, came off as saintly merciful.

Krampus sniffed the bars of the cage bearing darkening red stains. "Ummm. Tasty juices." His obscenely long tongue slithered between his lips to caress the bars clean.

Helga whimpered.

"Don't look," said Gunther.

Hans watched, waiting. When Krampus closed his eyes, savoring his ecstasy of flavor a trifle too much, Hans kicked. Between boot and bar he caught the round, fleshy tongue and ground it with twists as he would a viper against a stone.

Krampus yowled. The cage shook as he pushed against it to launch himself backwards, but his head stayed put. His eyes grew round. The cunning gone.

For a few moments, Hans held the wriggling tongue under his boot and glimpsed the mortality cowering in Krampus's soul.

The tongue slipped free and slurped back into the fiend's mouth. Krampus fell backward. His horns clopped on the stone floor and his head missed a sharp-edged stone by a hand's breadth.

Hans cursed their poor luck.

Krampus scrambled to his hooves. He screamed and gnashed his teeth. Waved his clawed hands—his regiment of bayonets—and shook his horns. His shadow from the fire leapt about on the wall like a dozen cavorting dancers.

The antics were reminiscent of a temper tantrum. If their situation were not so dire, Hans might have laughed, even so his lips twitched toward a grin at the small victory.

"You'll pay. You'll regret." Spittle flew as Krampus hissed the words which came out thick and clumsy as bread dough.

Krampus growled. He stomped to the front of the cave and there sat before the fire, feeding it from the fresh supply of faggots.

"What do we do?" whispered Gunther.

"It's three on one," said Hans. "And we can hurt him. If we fight him hard enough, he won't be able to get us out. Someone will come looking for us."

"We'll be hard-pressed to hold him off that long."

"We need weapons. Something to hit him with." Hans looked past the cage. The faggots, perfect batons, were out of reach, as were a few loose rocks. He turned to the wall, crisscrossed with cracks and fissures.

Hans cupped a hand to the side of his face. "Get loose rocks out of the wall."

The other two nodded. Sore fingers worked at cracks.

Hans periodically turned an eye toward Krampus. The fiend was not idle. He was fashioning supports for a spit from y-shaped branches. Hans dug harder for loose stones, ignoring the splits and tears in his fingernails.

JOHAN PRESSED HIS BACK against the church edifice. Secure in the shadows of the north tower, he watched the bonfire leap and fall, listened to it crackle. He studied those who tarried round it, drinking their hot frothy nogs and laughing with good cheer. He drew warmth from their presence even as the stone of their blessed church offered him devouring frost. Tonight of all nights was not one to be alone.

Father Mueller directed the feeding of the fire, shouting precise instructions for the tossing of each faggot. The priest gave orders like the sergeant-major of old. The man had been born centuries too late. He would have been an enthusiastic Knight Templar.

Johan stuffed what remained of the schneeballen he had swiped from old woman Heidrich's windowsill into his maw. Chewing slowly, he played his tongue over the buttery dough swathed in cinnamon and sugar. The pastry raised his thirst but he dared not ask for a nog and draw attention. He switched the bag to his other hand. The pair of gifts—little oblong boxes—shifted. Something for him to unwrap later.

The sanctuary would remain open tonight with candles burning. Johan was determined to spend the night there if he could avoid Father Mueller's detection. The good priest had not been a stranger to the mugs of nog. Had he not stumbled thrice already? To take sanctuary in the sanctuary. How fitting for the hunted and he did not doubt tonight he was hunted.

Johan's thoughts wandered to Krampus. Had the fiend visited his cottage yet, found the three brats in the loft? Probably. As much as he wanted to know, he had no intention of venturing anywhere near his home tonight. He had expected to see Helga come screaming that Krampus had taken her brother, mistaken him for another. What did her absence mean? And when would her parents miss her and her brother?

He pondered those questions, but not too deeply. All would be revealed in the days to come. What he did ponder was the indifference of these good people of good cheer. If they thought Krampus was coming for their plump children, they would be out in force with pitchforks and torches to hunt the monster down. They cared nothing for him. Johan got what he deserved, they would say. Hah! This year the joke was on them.

"HE'S COMING."

At the sound of Gunther's voice, Hans turned from his bare-handed mining. Krampus held a burning brand. He walked in a crouch. Wary. Some of his arrogance gone. The fire burned bright and hot. Gray smoke filled the upper reaches.

The roaring fire reminded Hans of hearth and home. Sweat clotted his eyebrows and threatened his eyes.

"What are you children doing there? Nothing naughty, I hope."

Hans noted the small pile of rock chips he had bought with his bloody fingertips and shredded nails. A far cry from the fist-sized rock he had hoped for, but some of the chips bore a sharp edge. Gunther and Helga had done no better. He selected the largest one with a sharp edge. No bigger than his thumb.

"I'll burn you." Krampus waved the torch at Hans.

"We'll hurt you," said Gunther. "Three of us."

Krampus hissed through his fangs. He focused on Gunther. An ugly smile contorted his red visage. "You're a marked one. You must be a very, very bad boy."

Gunther's retort—if he had one—died in his throat.

Krampus rushed the cage, roaring and waving the brand.

They flattened their backs to the wall. Instinct over thought. The cage protected them as much as it confined them.

"Stop fearing," said Hans. "We can't be afraid."

"Hee, hee," cackled the fiend. "You should be very, very afeared. Saint Nick brings you goodies. I make you into goodies." Krampus laid the brand behind him but in reach. He set to work on the knots securing the door.

Gunther looked to Hans, ready to spring forward to attack through the bars. Hans shook his head no. Better to wait for the open door he reasoned.

Helga turned between the two of them. Her lips parted, her blue eyes pleading.

Wait, mouthed Hans.

Krampus's fingers danced over the knots. His green eyes flicked between the children and his rope work.

Hans pressed the rock blade between his fingers. Sweat dampened his palms. It ran from under his arms to tickle his ribs. The shard's edge would cut like a razor he told himself.

The ropes fell loose. The door twitched, wanting to swing open. Krampus's gaze shifted between them. He reached behind, scratching his claws across the floor, feeling for the brand.

Hans crouched on the balls of his feet, coiled to lunge. Slash him. Rip his hide. Make him bleed. His mantra looped in his head.

Krampus waved the brand at Hans. The fire flared around the blackened end.

"Which one to eat first? I haven't tasted a girl in a long time."

Helga whimpered.

Krampus chortled.

"He won't get you," Hans said.

"Saint Nick has a soft spot for little girls." Krampus curled the fingers of his free hand around the bars of the door.

The fiend swept into the cage with preternatural speed.

The yellow flames were in Hans's face before he realized the door was open. The heat singed his eyebrows. The smoke from burning sap stung his sinuses. His head jerked backward, clopping the wall behind.

Helga screamed.

Hans slashed at the arm extending the brand. The edge slid across the shaggy blond hairs. No resistance. No hot blood gurgled onto his hand. He slashed again and harder again. The shard slipped like a skate over ice.

"Nooo!"

Gunther's cry came to Hans as through a memory, something from a nightmare. His hand slashed again and again with futile rage on its own volition. The dumb member knew not what else to do. His gaze took in Helga.

His sister swiped at the red mask of laughing evil inches out of her arm's reach. She screamed with each frantic swipe.

Krampus was not afraid. He knew his hair's strength.

Gunther squirmed, arms and legs flailing. Krampus gripped him by the neck.

With his arms outstretched to either side, Krampus left his center open.

Helga lunged into the gap. Her aim was not perfect. The knife edge of her shard cut across the bridge of the fiend's nose. It opened a gash below his eye. Blackish blood welled up along the line like a pot over boiling.

"Aaaiiiieeeee!"

A needle of sound stung his ears. Hans clapped both hands to the sides of his head. He screwed his eyes shut.

"Gunther! Gunther! He can't breathe." Helga's screams came through water.

Hans opened his eyes to a mad world.

Krampus held the door closed with his hairy back. Blood slicked the left side of his face. Some of it clotted in the hair on his neck, sticking together in thick globules of dark red. More puddled beside his hoof. He gripped Gunther by the neck in both hands. He snarled with the squeezing.

Gunther gurgled around his protruding tongue. His hands and feet twitched.

"Don't look." Hans threw himself over Helga. He caught sight of the brand. Still alight. Inside the cage. "Cover your eyes."

Helga sobbed. Hans didn't look to see if she obeyed.

He took up the brand. The fire had burned half of it by now and the heat singed his thumb. Ignoring the pain, he stabbed the brand through the bars and into the fiend's back. The blackened end crumbled to ash. The fire flamed, but the hair didn't catch.

Krampus snarled over his shoulder. His hands did not slacken their grip on Gunther's neck. With one side of his face bright red and the other blackish with blood, Krampus appeared a demented harlequin.

Hans stabbed Krampus again and again in the back. As with his earlier slashes to the fiend's arm, his efforts yielded nothing. His actions were madness, but anger and frustration drove him on.

He chanced to see Gunther's face, now bluish, cold with death as a glacier. The boy's eyes bulged. They were dull. His soul had departed. Gunther was dead. Hans had seen the moment enough in animals to know. The birthmark appeared to have faded. A trick of the light.

The death shocked Hans out of his madness. He couldn't burn the hair and he couldn't burn the knots, but the bars were plain wood. He shifted his grip on the diminishing brand. His thumb would blister.

He scurried to the far end of the cage where it met the wall. He engulfed a horizontal bar with flame. Krampus had wrapped several branches together with his hair which countered the fire, but the branches smoked with heat before catching.

Krampus shrieked. He dropped Gunther, whom he was strangling well beyond death, and took two steps toward Hans. Krampus stopped. He lunged back to the door.

Hans bit his lower lip in frustration. Helga might have escaped behind him. He moved the flame, leaving blackened bars behind.

Krampus tied the door, leaving long strands of hair to droop.

Hans suspected the knots were simpler and looser.

With the door secure, Krampus rushed toward Hans and thrust his hand ahead, grasping for the brand.

Hans pulled it away. He scooted to the wall out of reach.

Krampus snarled at him. Pain and anger seemed to deprive the fiend of speech.

"Helga! The knots on the door."

She shook her gaze from Gunther's lifeless form. After a few painfully frustrating moments, she caught onto her brother's meaning.

Krampus snarled at Helga. His body twitched in one direction and then the other as his gaze shifted between nimble fingers attacking the knots and a fire ready to burn the cage.

JOHAN HAD SLIPPED DEEPER into the shadows along the outer wall of the church. Snow fell in flakes the size of his thumb. He sat on the ground where two brick walls joined at a right angle, giving him some shelter and a view of the lane. The bonfire was dying, more smoke than flame. The wind carried the smoke with the snow, making strange bedfellows.

He pulled his knees up to his chest. Snow gathered on his hat, shoulders, and knees, giving him the look of a gargoyle. His legs and arms were stiffening with the cold.

The men at the bonfire had organized into groups of four to search the village and neighboring woods. The women were in the sanctuary. Their voices permeated the stained glass and settled on him like the snow. If they did not leave soon, Johan would have to find another place to spend the night.

The parents of Hans and Helga had finally missed their dear children.

HANS PRESSED HIS SISTER to his chest. Her hands covered her ears and her nose was buried in the wool of his sweater. She might hide from the sounds and smells, but she could not efface them. Hans had nowhere to hide.

The smokey aroma of roasting meat permeated the cave and nauseated him. He had been sick twice and felt hot bile rising again. Far worse than the smell was the sound of Krampus eating. The fiend had made a big show of tearing meat with his teeth, smacking his lips, and snapping bones to suck their marrow. He had slurped at his fingers so as not to waste the least drops of fat.

All the while, Krampus had mocked them, reminding the pair that one of them would be next.

The sounds of eating had mercifully ended. Hans scowled at the fiend sleeping against the cave wall near the entrance. Fresh snow had blown in and dusted the fiend's black hooves with delicate white crystals. His belly extended obscenely, a great lump that had once been Hans's friend. Krampus had not bothered to clean the blood from his face, which still bore the dual-colored visage of a harlequin.

Hans sniffed and wiped tears away with the back of his hand. This should not have happened. They were not Johan. The evil bully was somewhere in the village, laughing at their fate and his escape.

After the brand had stopped burning, Krampus had chased Helga from the knots and tightened them. Hans had not burned enough of the bars to break a hole. There had been nothing else for them to do but avert their senses from what followed. Krampus had chattered incessantly to ensure they did not forget what he was about.

Hans worried about Helga. The light had gone out of her eyes as sure as it had faded from Gunther's. She had given up. He feared she wouldn't have the will to fight when Krampus came again. And how could they fight?

"Krampus!"

Hans sat up. One arm fell away from Helga. The shout came from close outside. He dared not hope, but the voice carried the weight and force of a large man.

Had he imagined it? Krampus snored on in his gluttonous intoxication.

"KRAMPUS! I can smell you."

The fiend startled. "Saint Nick?"

"Help! Help!" Hans's hoarse voice cracked like dry leaves. There was no juice in his mouth or throat to grease it.

A white-bearded man wearing a fur hat of red fox fringed with ermine poked his head into the cave. He studied Krampus and then turned his attention to Hans and Helga. The man scowled.

Hans lunged to shake the bars of the cage. "Help! He's going to eat us."

"Steady." The man raised a mittened hand toward Hans. "No one's going to be eating you. Let's get this mess sorted."

Krampus had clambered to his hooves although his extended belly made balance difficult. "Mess? Sorted? What?"

The man squeezed his beaver-coat-wrapped bulk through the narrow cave entrance and then dragged a brown canvas bag behind. Something inside the bag kicked, punched, and whined to no effect.

"Yes, Krampus. This *mess*. Who are those children?"

Helga joined Hans at the bars. "Who is that?" she whispered. "Is he going to save us?"

"Krampus called him Saint Nick."

"Well, they're uh, well, one of them is Johan's sister." The explanation tumbled forth like a mountain stream under a springtime sun. "There were two boys and a girl in Johan's cottage and they wouldn't tell me who was Johan. I could tell they were lying. I couldn't leave them. Couldn't let such naughty children get away." Krampus looked from Saint Nick to the twitching bag and back. "I figured they were siblings and one bad apple they say so I figured I would save you the trouble and take 'em all at once."

Saint Nick clicked his tongue. "You did some thinking on your own, eh?"

Krampus nodded.

"You didn't scout the village or lay eyes on this Johan before tonight?"

Krampus hemmed and hawed.

"Did you?!" Saint Nick roared.

Fiend and children startled alike. Krampus cowered before Saint Nick more than the schoolchildren withered before the rod of Father Mueller.

"There were difficulties," Krampus whined. "I had to find a new cave."

"Did I tell you to take one and only one child? A very specific child?"

"Yes, but—"

"And how many did you take?"

"Three."

"One in your belly and those two in the cage?"

Krampus nodded.

"Ay yi yi. Why do I have to work with such idiots!" Saint Nick pointed at the squirming bag. "*This* is Johan. These are innocent children and if I'm right, the one you've eaten was the most kind and purely good child in the village!"

"But, but—" The color was draining from Krampus's face, leaving one side a light pink. "They tricked me."

"No, Krampus. Johan tricked you and you fell headfirst into the trap because you did not plan ahead." Saint Nick fumed, breathing heavily through his nose. His visage had taken on the red that Krampus had lost.

"Oh."

"You ate the wrong one. You know what that means."

"No. No!" Krampus pressed his hands to his twisting belly.

"And no more hunting for you for the next three seasons. Bad children will multiply like lemmings and grow to bad adults because of your incompetence."

Krampus fell on his hands and knees to disgorge his stomach contents into a steaming, watery pile of half-digested meat. He retched again and again. A putrid smell filled the cave.

Saint Nick wrinkled his nose and turned aside in disgust. Hans and Helga averted their gazes.

When the fiend's retching slowed to coughing and spitting, Saint Nick tapped his shoulder with a black, fur-covered boot.

"Let those two out."

Krampus bowed his head as he worked on the knots. His curled horns bobbed with the motion of his head as he groaned. Strings of vomit trailed from his mouth.

Hans allowed Helga to escape first. She scooted past Krampus without a backward glance. Hans cocked his right leg back and then kicked the fiend in the stomach, unleashing a swarm of spitting coughs.

"Steady," said Saint Nick.

Hans passed the twitching bag. He considered feeling sorry for Johan, for a moment, and then banished the thought. Gunther had died in Johan's place through trickery. As good as murder.

Saint Nick led them up the mountain to a level clearing where two reindeer hitched to a sleigh waited. The reindeer snorted, puffing clouds of condensation, as Saint Nick and the children crunched through fresh snow and the frozen layers beneath. The bells on the reindeers' tack jingled as they shook snow from their antlers.

"Were they sleeping?" said Helga.

"Whenever they can," said Saint Nick.

Hans and Helga climbed into the sleigh to sit on the bench in front of Saint Nick. A heavy, musky scent surrounded the reindeer. Hans had a thousand questions, but his tongue lay stuck in his mouth, cold and heavy as a dead ewe.

Saint Nick snapped the reigns. "Walk on."

The reindeer leaped. The sleigh followed, arcing over a stand of larch. The top of the tallest tree scraped the bottom of the sled.

"Oh well," said Saint Nick. "Wouldn't be the new year without new paint for the sleigh."

Hans and Helga gripped the bench. The sleigh tilted from side to side. Snow swirled into their faces. This should have been the highpoint of their young lives, but after the harrowing encounter with Krampus, the ride seemed anticlimactic.

Saint Nick said nothing to the reindeer but somehow guided the sleigh to a field near the children's farm.

"I'm sorry for all you suffered tonight. Krampus is, well—"

"He killed Gunther," said Helga.

"And both of you owe Gunther a great debt. It will weigh on your souls and I'm afraid it can never be repaid."

Hans considered his ineffectual slashing at Krampus's arm. He should have been the one to step in front of his sister, not Gunther. And two days before, he had betrayed him, let him suffer Johan's punishment with Father Mueller's rod.

"Yes, there may be a Saint Gunther someday." Saint Nick stared into the snowy sky.

The reindeer shook their necks and pawed the ground with their hooves. The snow fell thicker and faster now in that silent way that only snow can accumulate. Hans could barely discern the dark hulk of their farmhouse.

"You'll be wanting these. I found them with Johan." Saint Nick gave Hans the two small packages—Christmas presents for his parents. A day ago, he would have risked much to retrieve them. They no longer seemed very important.

"Thank you." Hans spoke mechanically, without meeting Saint Nick's gaze.

"Yes. And for both of you." Saint Nick pulled peppermint sticks out of his pocket and presented one each to Hans and Helga.

The reindeer snorted.

"Yes, yes. Don't get your antlers in a tangle." Saint Nick turned to the children. "It's been a long night and they want their oats."

The children climbed out of the sleigh.

"Thank you, sir," said Hans.

"Yes, thank you," echoed Helga.

Saint Nick snapped the reins. "Walk on."

The white-bearded man raised a mittened hand to them in farewell as the sleigh leapt into the snowy night.

"Merry Christmas," he called.

Dear Readers,

Thank you so much for reading *Krampus Comes to Town*. I had a lot of fun writing this tale and I hope you enjoyed reading it.

Stay up to date on my writing by visiting my website at jeffchapmanbooks.com[1] and joining my Readers Group.

Thanks for reading and I look forward to hearing your feedback in reviews or directly.

Have a great day,

Jeff

---

1.    http://jeffchapmanbooks.com/

# About the Author

Jeff Chapman writes software by day and speculative fiction when he should be sleeping. His tales range from fantasy to horror and they don't all end badly. He lives with his wife, children, and cats in a house with more books than bookshelf space.

You can find me on my Goodreads Author Page[1], on Facebook[2], or check out my website at jeffchapmanbooks.com[3].

WANT A COUPLE FREE ebooks? Want to stay up to date on new titles and special offers?

Consider subscribing to my Very Important Readers Group[4]. My short stories **"The Ivy and the Walnut"** and **"The Wand"** are *only* available to readers in my Readers Group.

Click here to get started: jeffchapmanbooks.com[5].

---

1.  http://www.goodreads.com/JeffChapman

2.  http://www.facebook.com/JeffChapmanWriter

3.  http://jeffchapmanbooks.com

4.  http://jeffchapmanbooks.com/

5.  http://jeffchapmanbooks.com/

# Don't miss out!

Visit the website below and you can sign up to receive emails whenever Jeff Chapman publishes a new book. There's no charge and no obligation.

https://books2read.com/r/B-A-YLKF-IBFKC

**BOOKS 2 READ**

Connecting independent readers to independent writers.

# Also by Jeff Chapman

**Comic Cat Tales**
The Cat Lady Is Always Right
A Cat Called Blackjack


**Huckster Tales**
The Black Blade


**The Cats of Incognito Lane**
Chasing the Great Corvid: An Incognito Lane Tale


**Standalone**
Last Request: A Victorian Gothic
Blood and Beauty and Other Weird Tales
Strange Paths to Wonder: Fantasy Stories
Krampus Comes to Town

Watch for more at https://www.jeffchapmanbooks.com/.